SMALL COUNTRY

a novel

GAËL FAYE

Translated from the French by Sarah Ardizzone

HOGARTH

LONDON · NEW YORK

Translation copyright © 2018 by Sarah Ardizzone

Published in the United States by Hogarth, an imprint of the Crown Publishing Group, a division of Penguin Random House LLC, New York. crownpublishing.com

HOGARTH is a trademark of the Random House Group Limited, and the H colophon is a trademark of Penguin Random House LLC.

Originally published in France as *Petit Pays* by Éditions Grasset in 2016. Copyright © Éditions Grasset & Fasquelle, 2016. Éditions Grasset is grateful to Catherine Nabakov for contributing to the publication of this work.

This book is supported by the Institut français du Royaume-Uni as part of the Burgess Programme.

Library of Congress Cataloging-in-Publication Data is available upon request.

ISBN 978-1-5247-5987-2
Ebook ISBN 978-1-5247-5989-6

Printed in the United States of America

Jacket design by Rachel Willey
Jacket photographs by (figure) Mwangi Kirubi; (landscape inside figure) Patrick Rudolph

10 9 8 7 6 5 4 3 2 1

First United States Edition

For Jacqueline

Prologue

I REALLY DON'T KNOW HOW THIS STORY BEGAN.

Papa tried explaining it to us one day in the pick-up truck.

"In Burundi, you see, it's like in Rwanda. There are three different ethnic groups. The Hutu form the biggest group, and they're short with wide noses."

"Like Donatien?" I asked.

"No, he's from Zaire, that's different. Like our cook, Prothé, for instance. There are also the Twa pygmies. But we won't worry about them, there are so few they hardly count. And then there are the Tutsi, like your mother. The Tutsi make up a much smaller group than the Hutu, they're tall and skinny with long noses and you can never tell what's going on inside their heads. Take you, Gabriel," he said, pointing at me, "you're a proper Tutsi: we can never tell what you're thinking."

I had no idea what I was thinking, either. What was anyone supposed to make of all that? So I asked a question instead:

"The war between Tutsis and Hutus . . . is it because they don't have the same land?"

"No, they have the same country."

"So . . . they don't have the same language?"

"No, they speak the same language."

"So, they don't have the same God?"

"No, they have the same God."

"So . . . why are they at war?"

"Because they don't have the same nose."

And that was the end of the discussion. It was all very odd. I'm not sure Papa really understood it, either. From that day on, I started noticing people's noses in the street, as well as how tall they were. When my little sister Ana and I went shopping in town, we tried to be subtle about guessing who was Hutu and who was Tutsi.

"The guy in white trousers is a Hutu," we would whisper, "he's short with a wide nose."

"Right, and the one towering over everybody in a hat, he's extra-skinny with a long nose, so he must be a Tutsi."

"See that man over there, in the striped shirt? He's a Hutu."

"No, he's not—look, he's tall and skinny."

"Yes, but he's got a wide nose!"

That's when we began to have our suspicions about this whole ethnic story. Anyway, Papa didn't want us talking about it. He thought children should stay out of politics. But we couldn't help it. The atmosphere was becoming stranger by the day. At school, fights broke out at the slightest provocation, with friends calling each other "Hutu" or "Tutsi" as an insult. When we were all watching *Cyrano de Bergerac*, one student was even overheard saying: "Look, with a nose like that he's *got* to be Tutsi." Something in the air had changed. And you could smell it, no matter what kind of nose you had.

I am haunted by the idea of returning. Not a day goes by without the country calling to me. A secret sound, a scent on the breeze, a certain afternoon light, a gesture, sometimes silence is enough to stir my childhood memories. "You won't find anything there, apart from ghosts and a pile of ruins," Ana keeps telling me. She refuses to hear another word about that "cursed country." I listen and I believe her. She's always been more clear-headed than me. So I put it out of my mind. I decide, once and for all, that I'm never going back. My life is here. In France.

Except that I no longer live anywhere. Living somewhere involves a physical merging with its landscape, with every crevice of its environment. There's none of that here. I'm passing through. I rent. I crash. I squat. My town is a dormitory that serves its purpose. My apartment smells of fresh paint and new linoleum. My neighbors are perfect strangers, we avoid each other politely in the stairwell.

I live and work just outside Paris. In Saint-Quentin-en-Yvelines. RER line C. This new town is like a life without a past. It took me years to feel "integrated." To hold down a stable job, an apartment, hobbies, friendships.

I enjoy connecting with people online. Encounters that last an evening or a few weeks. The girls who date me are all different, each one beautiful in her own way. I feel intoxicated listening to them, inhaling the fragrance of their hair, before surrendering to the warm oblivion of their arms, their legs, their bodies. Not one of them fails to ask me the same nagging question, and it's always on our first date: "So, where are you from?" A question as mundane as it is predictable. It feels like an obligatory rite of passage, before the relationship can develop any further. My skin—the color of caramel—must explain itself by offering up its pedigree. "I'm a human being." My answer rankles with them. It's not that I'm trying to be provocative. Any more than I want to appear pedantic or philosophical. But when I was just knee-high to a locust, I had already made up my mind never to define myself again.

The evening progresses. My technique is smooth. They talk. They enjoy being listened to. I am drunk. Deep in my cups. Drowning in alcohol, I shrug off sincerity. I become a fearsome hunter. I make them laugh. I seduce them. Just for fun, I return to the question of my roots, deliberately keeping the mystery alive. We play at cat-and-mouse. I inform them, with cold cynicism, that my identity can be weighed in corpses. They don't react. They try to keep things light. They stare at me with doe-like eyes. I want them. Sometimes, they give themselves up. They take me for a bit of a character. But I can entertain them for only so long.

I am haunted by the idea of returning but I keep putting it off, indefinitely. There's the fear of buried truths, of nightmares left on the threshold of my native land. For twenty years I've been going back there—in my dreams at night, in the magical thinking of my days—back to my neighborhood, to our street where I lived happily with my family and friends. My childhood has left its marks, and I don't know what to do about this. On good days, I tell myself it has made me strong and sensitive. But when I'm staring at the bottom of a bottle, I blame my childhood for my failure to adapt to the world.

My life is one long meandering. Everything interests me. Nothing ignites my passion. There's no fire in my belly. I belong to the race of slouchers, of averagely inert citizens. Every now and again I have to pinch myself. I notice the way I behave in company, at work, with my office colleagues. Is that guy in the lift mirror really me? The young man forcing a laugh by the coffee machine? I don't recognize him. I have come from so far that I still feel astonished to be here. My colleagues talk about the weather or what's on TV. I can't listen to them anymore. I'm having trouble breathing. I loosen my shirt collar. My clothes restrict me. I stare at my polished shoes: they gleam, offering a disappointing reflection. What has become of my feet? They're in hiding. I never walk barefoot outdoors these days. I wander over to the window. Under the low-hanging sky, through the gray sticky drizzle, there's not a single mango tree in the tiny park wedged between the shopping center and the railway lines.

This particular evening, on leaving work, I run for refuge to the nearest bar, opposite the station. I sit down by the table football and order a whiskey to celebrate my thirty-third birthday. I try ringing Ana, but she's not answering her mobile. I refuse to give up, redialing her number several times, until I remember she's on a business trip in London. I want to talk to her, to tell her about the phone call I received this morning. It must be a sign. I have to return, if only to be clear in my own mind. To bring this obsessive story to an end, once and for all. To close the door behind me. I order another whiskey. The noise from the television above the bar temporarily drowns out my thoughts. A twenty-four-hour news channel is broadcasting images of people fleeing war. I witness their makeshift boats washing up on European soil. The children who disembark are frozen, starving, dehydrated. Their lives played out on the global football pitch of insanity. Whiskey in hand, I watch them from the comfort of my VIP box. Public opinion holds that they've fled hell to find El Dorado. Bullshit! What about the country inside them?—nobody ever mentions that. Poetry may not be news. But it is all that human beings retain from their journey on this earth. I avert my gaze from images that capture reality, if not the truth. Perhaps those children will write the truth, one day. I'm as gloomy as a motorway service station in winter. Every birthday it's the same: this intense melancholy that comes crashing down on me like a tropical downpour when I think about Papa, Maman, my friends, and that never-ending party with the crocodile at the bottom of our garden . . .

I

I'LL NEVER KNOW THE TRUE CAUSE OF MY PARENTS'
separation. There must have been some fundamental misun-
derstanding from the outset—a manufacturing flaw in their
encounter, an asterisk nobody saw or wanted to see. Back then,
my parents were young and good-looking. Their hearts puffed
up with hope, like the sun that shone on African independ-
ence. What a sight! On their wedding day, Papa was astonished to have slipped a ring onto his beloved's finger. My father
didn't lack charm, of course, with his piercing green eyes, his
chestnut hair streaked with blond and his Viking stature. But
Maman was head and shoulders above him—even her ankles
were legendary! They hinted at long, lithe limbs that turned
women's stares into daggers and made men dream of half-open
shutters. Papa was a young Frenchman from the Jura who had
arrived in Africa by accident, for his voluntary service, and
who came from a village set in mountains that bore a striking
resemblance to the Burundian countryside. Except that, back
where he came from, none of the women could compete with
Maman's elegance, there were no slender freshwater reeds, no
beauties slim as skyscrapers with ebony skin and eyes as wide as
those of the Ankole cattle. What music! On their wedding day,
a careless rumba escaped some out-of-tune guitars as happiness
crooned *cha-cha-cha* numbers beneath a sky pricked with stars.

They could see it all. What mattered was this: Loving. Living. Laughing. Being. Forging ahead, never faltering, to the ends of the earth, and even beyond.

The trouble was that my parents were two lost teenagers suddenly asked to grow into responsible adults. Scarcely had they left behind the hormones and sleepless nights of puberty than it was time to clear away the drained bottles, empty the ashtrays of joint butts, put the psychedelic rock records back into their sleeves, and fold up their bell-bottomed trousers and Indian shirts. A bell had tolled, signaling the arrival—too sudden, too soon—of children, taxes, worries, and responsibilities. Alongside these came growing uncertainty, rampant banditry, dictators and military coups, Structural Adjustment Programmes, forgotten ideals, and mornings that struggled to break, the sun lingering in bed a little longer each day. Reality had struck. And it was a cruel blow. Their carefree beginnings transformed into a rhythm as tyrannical as the relentless ticking of a clock. What had come so naturally at first was now backfiring on my parents, as it dawned on them that they had confused desire with love, and that each of them had invented qualities in the other. It turned out they hadn't shared dreams, merely illusions. True, each of them had nurtured a dream, but it amounted to nothing more than their own selfish hopes, with neither of them ready to fulfill the other's expectations.

Still, back then, before all that, before this story I'm about to tell, ours was a happy, uncomplicated existence. Life was the way it was, the way it had always been, the way I wanted it to stay. A gentle, peaceful slumber, no mosquito dancing in my ear, no deluge of questions drumming on the corrugated iron of my head. In those happy times, if anyone asked me, "Life's good?" I would always answer: "Life's good!" Wham-bam. When you're happy, you don't think twice about it. It was only afterward that I began to consider the question. Weighing up the pros and cons. Being evasive, as I nodded vaguely. And it wasn't just me—the whole country was at it. People only ever replied with: "Not bad." Because life could no longer be altogether good, after everything that had happened to us.

2

THE BEGINNING OF THE END OF OUR HAPPY DAYS GOES
back, I think, to that Feast of Saint-Nicholas, out on Jacques's
large terrace in Bukavu, Zaire. Once a month we paid old
Jacques a visit, it had become our tradition. Maman joined us
that day, although she had barely said a word to Papa in several
weeks. Before setting off, we went to the bank to pick up some
local currency. "We're millionaires!" said Papa as we left the
building. In Mobutu's Zaire, hyperinflation meant paying for a
glass of water with banknotes of five million zaires.

The border checkpoint marked our entry into another
world. Burundian restraint gave way to Zairean commotion.
In the unruly crowd, people greeted one another, heckled or
hurled abuse as if at a cattle market. Dirty, noisy kids eyed up
wing mirrors, windscreen wipers, and hubcaps splattered from
stagnant puddles, calculating their street value; grilled goat-
meat skewers—*brochettes*—were up for grabs in exchange for
a few wheelbarrows of cash; young mothers, zigzagging between the tailbacks of goods vehicles and minibuses jammed
bumper to bumper, hawked bags of spicy peanuts, and hard-
boiled eggs for dipping in coarse salt; beggars, with legs cork-
screwed by polio, pleaded for a few million zaires to help them
survive the unfortunate consequences of the fall of the Ber-
lin Wall; and a preacher standing on the hood of his battered

Mercedes, wielding a Swahili Bible bound in royal python skin, announced the end of the world at the top of his voice. Inside his rusty sentry box, a dozing soldier waved a fly-swatter in desultory fashion, the stench of diesel combining with hot air to parch the throat of one more long-term unpaid functionary. On the roads, vast craters spawned from old potholes gave the cars a bumpy ride. Not that this prevented the customs officer from meticulously inspecting each vehicle, checking tire tread depth or engine water levels, as well as ensuring that the indicators were in good working order. In the event of the car or truck failing to produce any of these desired shortcomings, the customs officer would insist on a certificate of baptism or first communion to qualify for entry into the country.

Papa was battle-weary that afternoon and in the end paid the bribe all those ludicrous checks had really been about. The barrier rose at last and we drove on through the steam from the hot-water springs dotted along the side of the road.

After the small town of Uvira and before Bukavu we stopped off at some roadside *gargotes* to buy banana doughnuts and paper cones of fried ants. There were all kinds of fantastical signs advertizing these cheap eateries: *Au Fouquet's des Champs-Elysées . . . Snack-bar Giscard d'Estaing . . . Restaurant fête comme chez vous . . .* When Papa took out his Polaroid camera to capture the local spirit of inventiveness, Maman sucked her teeth and berated him for marveling at an exoticism concocted for whites.

After nearly running over a multitude of roosters, ducks, and children, we arrived in Bukavu—a sort of Garden of Eden on the banks of Lake Kivu and an art deco relic of a town that had once been Futurist. At Jacques's house the table had already been laid to welcome us. He had ordered in fresh prawns from Mombasa.

"They're no match for oysters," declared Papa, in his element, "but it's good to eat something decent every once in a while!"

"What are you complaining about, Michel? Do we feed you badly at home?" Maman asked coldly.

"Yes! That idiot Prothé makes me swallow his starchy African cooking every lunchtime. If only he knew the correct way to grill entrecôte!"

"Don't get me started, Michel!" said Jacques, taking up the theme. "My baboon in the kitchen grills everything to death, with the excuse that it kills off parasites. I've forgotten what rare steak tastes like. I'll be glad to get back to Brussels and dose myself up on amoeba!"

Everyone burst out laughing except for Ana and me, at the far end of the table. I was ten, and she was seven, which probably explains why we didn't appreciate Jacques's sense of humor. In any case, we were strictly forbidden to speak unless spoken to. This was the golden rule when we were taken somewhere. Papa couldn't abide children joining in grown-up conversations. Especially not when we were visiting Jacques, who was like a second father to him: a role model to the point that, without even realizing it, Papa would often copy Jacques's expressions, his body language, and even the cadence of his voice. "He's the one who taught me everything I know about Africa!" Papa would often tell Maman.

Ducking his head under the table to get out of the wind, Jacques lit a cigarette with his silver Zippo that was engraved with two stags. Then he stood up and stared at Lake Kivu for a moment, a few curls of smoke escaping his nostrils. From his terrace, you could make out a string of tiny islets in the distance. Beyond them, on another of the lake's shores, was the city of Cyangugu in Rwanda. Maman's gaze was set in that direction. Her thoughts must have weighed her down every time we ate at Jacques's place. Rwanda, her country, which she had left in 1963 during a night of massacres, by the light of the flames that had set her family home ablaze, the country where she had never again set foot since the age of four, was right there, a few cable lengths away, almost within reach.

Jacques's lawn was immaculately maintained by an elderly gardener who wielded his machete in great pendulum strokes, as if executing a golf swing. In front of us, in a stunning choreography, metallic-green hummingbirds gathered nectar from the red hibiscus flowers. A pair of crowned cranes strolled in the shade of the lemon and guava trees. Teeming with life and bursting with colors, Jacques's garden gave off a gentle scent of lemongrass. His house, which had been built using porous black rock from the volcano of Mount Nyiragongo and rare wood from the Nyungwe forest, resembled a Swiss chalet.

Jacques rang the small bell on the table and the cook appeared instantly, his uniform of a chef's toque and white apron clashing with his bare cracked feet.

"Bring us three bottles of Primus and clear up this goddamn mess!" Jacques ordered.

"How are you, Evariste?" Maman asked the cook.

"Thanks be to God, not too bad, Madame!"

"Leave God out of it!" Jacques retorted. "Things aren't too bad because there are still a few whites left in Zaire to keep the wheels turning. Without me, you'd be begging on the streets like the rest of your kind!"

"When I say God, I mean you, Boss!" the cook replied mischievously.

"Don't make fun of me, you baboon!"

The pair of them cackled.

"And to think I couldn't hold onto a good woman for more

than three days," Jacques went on, "but I've been lumbered with this chimpanzee for thirty-five years!"

"You should have married me, Boss!"

"*Funga kimwa!* Go and find us those beers instead of talking goddamn rubbish!" Jacques guffawed again, before producing a hawking that made me want to bring my prawns back up.

The cook set off, humming something liturgical. Jacques blew his nose vigorously into a handkerchief embroidered with his initials, picked up his cigarette once more, dropped some ash on the polished parquet floor, and turned to Papa.

"The last time I was in Belgium, the docs told me to give up the smokes or I was done for. There's nothing I haven't been through here: wars, looting, shortages, Bob Denard and Kolwezi, thirty years of bloody 'Zairinization,' and it's the cigarettes that'll get me in the end! Goddamn it!"

Age-spots flecked his hands and balding head. It was the first time I'd seen him wearing shorts. His hairless, milky-white legs contrasted with the burned skin of his forearms and his sun-etched face; it was as if his body had been assembled from ill-assorted pieces.

"Those doctors might have a point, you know, you should slow down," said Maman, sounding worried. "Three packets a day is a lot, Jacques."

"Don't you start as well," Jacques directed his words at Papa as if Maman weren't there. "My father smoked like a trooper and he lived to ninety-five. You don't know the half of the life he led. Back in the days of Leopold II, the Congo was a whole different story! A great strapping man, my father! He built the Kabalo–Kalemi railway line. It hasn't worked in a long time, by the way, that line, like the rest of this messed-up country. What a goddamn shambles!"

"Why don't you sell up? Come and settle in Bujumbura.

You could have yourself a nice life over there," said Papa, with an enthusiasm he reserved for spur-of-the-moment ideas. "I've got plenty of construction sites, and I'm being asked to tender for more contracts than I can keep track of. Right now, there's money for the making!"

"Sell up? Stop talking bullshit! My sister keeps phoning me about joining her in Belgium. 'Come back home, Jacques,' she says, 'it'll turn out badly for you. When it comes to Zaireans, the whites always end up getting robbed and lynched.' Can you picture me in an apartment in Ixelles? I've never lived over there, so what the hell would I do in some boring rich suburb of Brussels, at my age? The first time I set foot in Belgium, I was twenty-five with two bullets in my belly, sustained in an ambush while we were chasing the communists out of Katanga. I went under the surgeon's knife, they stitched me up, and I was back here double-quick. I'm more Zairean than any of those darkies. I was born here and I'll die here! I can handle Bujumbura for a few weeks, I sign two or three contracts, help out some big *bwanas*, do the rounds, catch up with old friends, and then I head home. Truth is, the Burundians don't do it for me. At least with the Zaireans, they're easy to understand: you just pay the bribe. One *matabish-bakshish* and things get moving! With the Burundians? Those people! They scratch their left ear with their right hand . . ."

"That's what I'm always telling Michel," said Maman. "I'm sick of Burundi, too."

"It's not the same, Yvonne," Papa snapped. "You dream of living in Paris, you're obsessed with the idea."

"Too right I am; it would suit you, it would suit me, and it would suit the children. What kind of future do we have in Bujumbura, apart from this lousy existence? Can you tell me that?"

"Give it a rest! It's your country you're talking about."

"Oh no, no, no, no, no . . . my country is Rwanda! Over there, right in front of you. Rwanda. I'm a refugee, Michel. And I always have been, in Burundian eyes. They make it very clear, with their insults and insinuations, their quotas for foreigners and restricted intakes in schools. So allow me to have my own opinion on Burundi!"

"Listen, darling," said Papa, trying to sound conciliatory. "Take a look around you. The mountains, the lakes, the nature. We live in a nice house, we have staff, we have space for the children, we enjoy a decent climate, and business is good. What else d'you want? You'd never have this kind of lifestyle in Europe. Trust me, it's far from the paradise you imagine. Why d'you think I've spent the last twenty years building my life here? Why d'you think Jacques would rather stay on than go home to Belgium? Here, we're privileged. There, we'd be nobodies. Why won't you hear that?"

"Talk all you like, Michel, but I know the other side of the story. Where you see gently undulating hills, I see the poverty of the people who live there. Where you marvel at the beautiful lakes, I'm already breathing in the methane that sleeps below those waters. You fled the peace and quiet of your France to seek out adventure in Africa. Good for you! I want the security I never had, the comfort of raising my children in a country where I'm not afraid of dying just because I'm—"

"Stop right there, Yvonne, I've had enough of your anxieties and your persecution complex. You always have to make a drama out of everything. You've got a French passport now, so what are you afraid of? You live in a villa in Bujumbura, not in a refugee camp, so please, cut it out!"

"I couldn't care less about your passport, it doesn't change anything, least of all the threats that are all around us. You've never been interested in my version of the story, Michel . . . You came here from Europe in search of a playground where you could eke out the dreams of your spoiled childhood in the West . . ."

"What are you talking about? You drive me crazy! Plenty of African women would give their eye teeth for what you have . . ."

Maman fixed Papa with such a hard look he didn't dare finish his sentence.

"Poor Michel," she went on calmly, "you don't even realize what you're saying anymore. A word of advice: Don't try your hand at racism when you're an old hippy at heart, it doesn't suit you. Leave that to Jacques and the real settlers."

Jacques choked on his cigarette. But Maman, who was beyond caring, stood up, flung her napkin in Papa's face, and stormed off. Just then the cook appeared, with a cheeky smile on his lips and the bottles of Primus on a plastic tray.

"Yvonne! Come back right now! Apologize to Jacques this minute!" bellowed my father, hovering over his seat with his fists clenched on the table.

"Leave it, Michel," said Jacques. "That's women for you . . ."

3

IN THE DAYS THAT FOLLOWED, PAPA TRIED SEVERAL times to make it up to Maman with sweet talk and jokes that left her cold. One Sunday, on a whim, he decided to take us out for lunch in Resha, by the shores of Lake Tanganyika, sixty kilometers from Bujumbura. It was to be our last Sunday, all four of us together, as a family.

The car windows were open wide and the wind made such a din it was almost impossible to hear one another. Maman seemed in her own world, and Papa kept trying to fill the silence with endless explanations that nobody had asked for.

"Look, over there, that's a kapok tree, as introduced by the Germans into Burundi at the end of the nineteenth century. It produces silk cotton, the fiber used for stuffing pillows."

The road ahead followed the lake and continued south all the way to the Tanzanian border.

"Tanganyika contains the most fish and, at over six hundred kilometers, is also the longest lake in the world," Papa went on for his own benefit. "It has a surface area larger than that of Burundi."

The rainy season was coming to a close and the sky was clear. We could see the corrugated-iron rooftops glinting on the mountains of Zaire, fifty kilometers away, on the other side of the lake. Tiny white clouds hung above the ridges, like balls of cotton wool.

The bridge over the Mugere river had collapsed after the recent floods, so we drove across the riverbed instead. Water began seeping into our jeep, and Papa activated the four-wheel drive system for the first time since buying the Pajero. When we arrived in Resha, a sign declared "Restaurant Le Castel." A narrow dirt track lined with mango trees led to the car park, where we were welcomed by a group of green monkeys grooming one another. At the entrance to the restaurant—an odd building with a red corrugated roof and a semaphore flag on top—there was a copper plaque depicting the Pharaoh Akhenaton.

We sat out on the terrace, under an Amstel parasol. Only one other table was taken, near the bar, by a minister having lunch with his family and flanked by two armed soldiers. The minister's children were even more well behaved than we were, scarcely moving or reaching for the Fanta bottles set down before them. A pair of loudspeakers crackled, feebly relaying a cassette by Canjo Amiss, while Papa rocked on his plastic chair and turned his keys on his finger. Maman was watching Ana and me with a sad smile. Then the waitress arrived and it was time to give our order: "Captain's *brochettes*, four! Two Fruito. Two Amstel." Maman never wasted words on restaurant staff, she sent telegrams instead. Waiters didn't warrant the benefit of verbs.

It wasn't unusual for the food to take at least an hour to arrive. The atmosphere at the table was heavy going, between Papa's clinking keys and Maman's fake smile, so Ana and I made ourselves scarce by diving head first into the lake. "Hey, kids, watch out for the crocs!" Papa roared, to scare us. Ten meters from shore a rock rose above the water, like the rounded back of a hippopotamus. We raced over to it, before swimming to the metal jetty from where we could dive and view the fish basking in the turquoise waters between the big rocks. As I climbed the ladder I spotted Maman on the beach, all in white, with her wide brown leather belt and a red scarf in her hair. She was waving at us to come and eat lunch.

After the meal, Papa drove us to the Kigwena forest to see the baboons. We walked for nearly an hour along a clay path without spotting anything, except for a few green turacos. There was no let-up in the tension between Maman and Papa: they didn't speak to each other and kept avoiding eye contact. My shoes got caked with mud. Ana ran ahead to find the monkeys before anyone else.

Next, Papa took us to Rumonge to visit the palm-oil factory for which he'd overseen the construction when he first arrived in Burundi in 1972. The machines were old and the entire building appeared to be coated in a greasy substance. Piles of palm nuts were drying on large blue sheets of tarpaulin. A vast palm grove extended for kilometers all around. While Papa was explaining the different stages of pressing nuts, I noticed Maman heading to the car. Later, back on the road, she closed the windows and turned on the air-conditioning. She put on a Khadja Nin tape and Ana and I started singing "Sambolera." Maman joined in. There was a beautiful quality to her voice, one that touched your soul, triggering as many goosebumps as the air-con. It made you want to pause the cassette and only listen to her.

Driving through the market at Rumonge, Papa changed gears and then tried to put his hand on Maman's knee. She batted him away, much as you might swat a fly from your plate. Papa immediately checked in the rear-view mirror and

I looked out of my window, pretending I hadn't seen anything. After thirty-two kilometers, Maman bought several balls of *ubusagwe* (a cold pastry made from cassava flour), which were rolled in banana leaves. We loaded them into the trunk. Toward the end of the trip, we stopped off at the Livingstone–Stanley Monument, which read "Livingstone, Stanley, 25-XI-1889." Ana and I messed about re-enacting the explorers' famous meeting: "Doctor Livingstone, I presume?" In the distance, I could see Papa and Maman finally talking to each other. I felt hopeful that they would make up, that Papa would wrap his strong arms around her and she would lay her head on his shoulder as they strolled, hand in hand like lovers, through the banana plantation below. But it wasn't long before I realized, from their angry gestures and jabbing fingers, that they were arguing. A warm wind prevented me from hearing what they were saying. The banana trees swayed, a pod of pelicans flew over the headlands and the red sun plunged behind the high plateaus to the west as a blinding light covered the glistening surface of the lake.

THAT NIGHT, the walls of our house trembled with Maman's rage. I heard the sounds of breaking glass, of windows being shattered and plates smashing on the floor.

"Yvonne, calm down," Papa kept pleading with her. "You'll wake up the entire neighborhood!"

"Fuck you!"

Raw emotion had transformed Maman's voice into a torrent of mud and gravel. A flood of words, a roar of insults filled the night. The noises were moving about our property: I could hear Maman howling below my window, then destroying the car windscreen. After that, silence, until the violence began rumbling again, all around. I watched my parents' footsteps to-ing and fro-ing in the light that filtered under my bedroom door. My little finger worried at a hole in the mosquito net over my bed. Their voices were indistinguishable, distorted by the high and low notes bouncing off the tiles and reverberating in the false ceiling, I could no longer tell what was French and what Kirundi, what was shouting and what were tears, whether these were my parents battling or the neighborhood dogs fighting to the death. I clung to my happy existence for the last time, but no matter how hard I tried to stop it from escaping, it was coated in the same palm oil that had glistened at the factory in Rumonge, and it slipped through my fingers. Yes, this was to be our last Sunday, all four of us together, as a family. That night, Maman left our house, Papa held back his tears and, while Ana was sleeping with clenched fists, my little finger tore the netting that had always protected me from mosquitoes.

4

TO MAKE MATTERS WORSE, IT WAS ALMOST CHRISTMAS. After an argument between Papa and Maman over who would have us for the holidays, it was agreed I would stay with Papa while Ana went with Maman to visit Eusébie, one of Maman's aunts who lived in Kigali. This would be the first time Maman had been back to Rwanda since 1963. The situation seemed more stable now, thanks to new peace agreements between the government and the Rwandan Patriotic Front, the rebels of Maman's generation who were themselves the sons and daughters of exiles.

Papa and I spent Christmas together, just the two of us. My present was a red BMX bike with multicolored tassels on the handles. I was so excited that, at first light on Christmas morning and before Papa was awake, I took it to show the twins who lived in the house opposite, at the entrance to our street. They were suitably impressed. We messed about doing *tchélélés*—skids—in the gravel. Then Papa appeared in his striped pajamas, livid, and dished out a slap, in full view of my friends, for leaving the house so early without permission. I didn't cry, or perhaps I did a little, but my tears were from the dust kicked up by our skids, or else a fly caught in my eye, I can't remember now.

For New Year's Day, Papa decided to take me on a hike through the Kibira forest. We spent the night in a village of pygmy potters, at an altitude of more than two thousand three hundred meters. The temperature was close to zero. At midnight, Papa let me have a few sips of banana beer to help warm me up, and to celebrate the start of 1993. Then we lay down together on the beaten earth, snuggled up by the fire.

Papa and I tiptoed out of the hut at dawn, while the pygmies snored on, their heads resting on the calabashes they used for drinking *urwagwa*, the local banana beer. Outside, the ground was covered in hoarfrost, the dew transformed into white crystals as a thick fog shrouded the tops of the eucalyptus trees. We followed a winding path through the forest. I found a large black-and-white beetle on a rotten trunk and popped it inside a metal box, making it the first specimen in my insect collection. As the sun rose gradually in the sky, the cool of dawn gave way to a dusty humidity. Papa walked in front of me, in silence, sweat turning his hair lank but frizzy just above the neck. The cries of baboons rang out through the forest. From time to time I was startled by something moving in the undergrowth, probably a serval cat or a civet.

Toward the end of the day we crossed paths with a group of pygmies, accompanied by a pack of basenji hunting dogs. They were from the village of blacksmiths, higher up in the mountains, and returning from a hunting expedition. They wore their bows slung across their shoulders, and their haul included the corpses of moles, Gambian pouched rats, and a chimpanzee. Papa was fascinated by these diminutive men who had maintained the same way of life for thousands of years. When we left them, his voice was tinged with sadness as he talked to me about the inevitable disappearance of their world because of modern life, progress, and Christian missions.

On the final stretch of track before we returned to the car, Papa asked me to stop.

"Go over there!" he said, producing a disposable camera. "I'll take a photo of you, as a souvenir."

I climbed a tree shaped like a giant catapult and stood between the two trunks, while Papa turned the little notched wheel. *Smile!* There was a *click* followed by the *whirr* of the film rewinding.

Back in the village, we thanked the pygmies for their welcome and hospitality. The kids ran behind our car for several kilometers, trying to grab hold of it until we reached the asphalt road. As we headed down to Bugarama, we were overtaken by the "suicide-bananas": bikers who pedaled as fast as the cars, their racks laden with heavy clusters of bananas or sacks of coal weighing in at tens of kilos. At that speed, a fall could prove fatal and the slightest swerve meant you might end up at the bottom of a precipice—in the cemetery of Tanzanian trucks and crushed minibuses. On the other side of the road the same cyclists, having delivered their wares to the capital, were climbing back up the mountain by discreetly holding onto the rear bumpers of the trucks. I tried to picture myself on my red BMX with its colorful tassels careering round the bends from Bugarama, overtaking cars and trucks in a crazy race, with the twins, Armand and Gino, cheering me on my arrival in Bujumbura, as if I'd just won the Tour de France.

It was dark when we arrived home. Papa tooted the horn several times in front of our gates that bore the sign: "Beware of the dog! *Imbwa Makali.*" The gardener limped over to open up, followed by our small russet-and-white curly-haired dog, a chance-cross between a bichon Maltese and a ratter, whose heart wasn't in playing his role as advertized.

"Where's Calixte?" Papa asked the gardener, stepping out of the car. "How come it's you opening the gates?"

"Calixte has vanished, Boss."

The dog was still following the gardener. He didn't have a tail, so he wagged his hindquarters as a sign of contentment. He also bared his gums, which made it look as if he were smiling.

"What do you mean, vanished?"

"He left very early this morning, and he won't be coming back."

"What are you talking about?"

"There've been a few problems with Calixte, Boss. Yesterday, we celebrated New Year's. While I was asleep, he went into the storehouse and stole a lot of gear. Then, he vanished . . . That's all I can tell you."

"What did he steal?"

"A wheelbarrow, a toolbox, a grinder, a soldering iron, two cans of paint . . ."

The gardener was in full flow with his list, but Papa stopped him with his hand.

"All right! All right! I'll register a complaint on Monday."

"He also stole Monsieur Gabriel's bicycle," the gardener added.

I felt sick to my stomach. No way. Surely Calixte would never do something like that? I was crying real tears now. It felt as if the whole world was against me.

"Don't worry, Gaby," Papa kept saying, "we'll find your bike."

5

THE FOLLOWING SUNDAY, THE DAY BEFORE SCHOOL began, Ana came back from Rwanda. Maman dropped her off at the house in the early afternoon. Ana's hair had been plaited into fine braids with blond highlights. Papa didn't approve, he thought the color was vulgar for a little girl. He argued with Maman, who immediately started up her motorbike and drove off, before I'd even had the chance to give her a kiss or wish her a happy New Year. I stood on the steps by the front door for the longest time, convinced that she'd be back as soon as she realized she had forgotten me.

Then the twins came over to tell me about their Christmas holidays at their grandmother's place in the countryside.

"It was horrible! There was no bathroom, so we had to wash stark naked in the courtyard in front of everybody. We swear, in God's name, Gaby!"

"And they're not used to seeing anyone mixed race, so the kids from the village came to spy on us through the fencing. 'Little white butts!' they kept shouting. How mean is that? Mamie shooed them away by throwing stones at them."

"That's when she noticed we weren't circumcized."

"D'you even know what circumcized means?"

I shook my head.

"It means snipping your willy!"

"So our grandmother asked our uncle to circumcize us."

"We didn't know what it meant, either. So, to begin with, we weren't really bothered. Mamie was speaking to Tonton Sosthène in Kirundi, and we couldn't understand what they were saying, but she kept pointing at our trouser flies. We wanted to call our parents, because we had a feeling that our grandmother and uncle were up to no good. The trouble is, it's the countryside where they live, for real, no telephone, no electricity. The toilets are a hole in the ground with long-stay flies parked up everywhere! In God's name!"

Every time they swore, the twins said "In God's name" and drew a finger across their neck, like a knife slitting a chicken's throat, before clicking in the air, thumb against index, *snap!*

"Tonton Sosthène turned up with our older cousins, Godefroy and Balthazar. They took us to the edge of the village, and into a small earth house with a wooden table in the middle of the room."

"Tonton had bought a razor blade in the shop."

"Godefroy held my arms behind my back while Balthazar blocked my legs. And then Tonton Sosthène pulled my pants down. He caught hold of my willy, put it on the table, unwrapped the Gillette, tugged on the skin and *sniiip!* He cut off the end! Then he put salt water on it to disinfect it. I swear, in God's name!"

"*Yébabawé!* I'm telling you, when I saw that I ran for the hills, like an impala being chased by leopards. But the cousins caught me, pinned me down, and *sniiip!* Same thing!"

"Afterward, Tonton Sosthène put our willy skins in a matchbox that he gave to Mamie. She opened the box to check the job had been done properly. You could see 'Satisfaction' by the Rolling Stones written on her face, in God's name! It was evil! To top it all, she buried our willy skins on her plot of land, under the banana trees!"

"Our willy skins have gone up to heaven! May God rest their souls!"

"Amen!"

"But that wasn't the last of it! No, we had to wear dresses, like girls, because—get this—trousers would rub you where the wound is."

"Wearing a dress was, like, an international embarrassment!"

"When our parents came to collect us at the end of the holidays, they were surprised by our outfits. Our father asked us what we were doing in skirts."

"We told him the whole story. Papa was furious with Mamie, he insisted we were French, not Jewish!"

"But our mother tried explaining it was for hygiene reasons. To prevent any dirt from getting stuck inside."

The twins were always out of breath by the time they got to the end of one of their stories. They gesticulated wildly to explain and bring drama to the tiniest detail. A deaf person could have understood them. When they spoke, it was a helter-skelter of words and a pile-up of phrases. As soon as one of them finished a sentence, the other one took over, like the baton change in a relay race.

"I don't believe you!" I told them.

Because, the fact was, the twins had a habit of lying. If one of them started fibbing, the other would keep going, even though they hadn't planned it. They had the gift of the gab. My father always said they were tall-story merchants, prestidigitators of the truth. When I told them I thought they were having me on, they choroused, "We swear, in God's name!" Then they drew a finger across their necks and clicked in the air, index against thumb, *snap*! They dropped their pants at the same time to reveal two little stubs of purplish-red meat. I shut my eyes in disgust.

"And you know what?" they added, pulling up their pants. "In our grandmother's village we saw someone riding your bike. We swear, in God's name!"

6

"Gaby! Gaby!"

Papa's hoarse voice woke me. I leaped out of bed, worried I'd be late for school. I often failed to wake up and Papa had to call me. Ana, by contrast, was always ahead of the game and dressed, with clips in her neatly brushed hair, coconut butter applied to her body, teeth cleaned and shoes polished. She would even remember to put her gourd in the fridge the night before, so that her water was nice and cool in the morning. She handed in her homework early and learned her lessons off by heart. What a girl! She always felt like my older sister, despite being three years younger. When I made it out into the hallway, I saw that Papa's bedroom door was closed. He was still asleep. Once again I'd fallen into the trap: the parrot had been mimicking him.

I headed out to sit on our *barza*, the covered terrace opposite the birdcage. Our parrot was pecking at peanuts by gripping them in his claws, then using his hooked beak to crush the shells and extract the seeds. He glanced at me, a black pupil in a yellow eye, before whistling the opening bars of the "Marseillaise," which Papa had taught him. He poked his head between the bars of the cage for me to stroke him. When my fingers sank into his gray plumage I could feel the hot pink flesh of his neck.

In the courtyard, a gaggle of geese ambled in single file past the night watchman who was crouched on his mat, a thick gray blanket pulled up to his chin, as he listened to a small radio that broadcast the morning news in Kirundi. Prothé came through the gates and walked up the path, climbing the three steps to the terrace to greet me. He had lost a lot of weight and while he had always looked older than his years, his gaunt features now made him resemble an old man. He hadn't come to work for the past few weeks because of the cerebral malaria that had nearly finished him off. Papa had paid all the medical bills, as well as his sessions with a traditional healer. I followed Prothé into the kitchen, where he changed out of his town clothes and into his work outfit: a threadbare shirt, trousers that were too short for him, and a pair of fluorescent plastic sandals.

"Would you prefer an omelet or a fried egg, Monsieur Gabriel?" he asked, inspecting the fridge.

"Two fried eggs please, Prothé."

Ana and I were already sitting on the *barza*, waiting for our breakfast, when Papa appeared with a few small cuts to his face and the remains of some shaving cream behind his left ear. On a large tray, Prothé brought out a Thermos of tea, a pot of honey, a saucer of powdered milk, margarine, gooseberry jam, and my fried eggs, slightly crispy, just the way I liked them.

"Morning, Prothé!" said Papa, noticing his employee's sallow complexion.

The cook nodded shyly.

"Looks like you're doing better!"

"Yes, I am, thank you, Monsieur. Thank you for your help. My family is very grateful to you. We pray for you, Monsieur."

"Don't thank me. As you know, the money I paid for your treatment will be docked from next month's wages," said Papa, matter-of-factly.

Prothé's face hardened. He picked up the tray and disappeared into the kitchen as Donatien arrived on the terrace with a rolling gait. He was in an *abacost*, the jacket worn without a shirt or a tie that Mobutu had imposed on Zaireans to free them from the colonial style; this one was short-sleeved and lightweight, in a dark fabric. Donatien had been Papa's foreman for twenty years, and was his most loyal employee. The workers on the construction sites called him *mzee*, the elder, although he was no more than forty. Donatien was from Zaire and had come to Burundi straight after his baccalaureate to work in the palm-oil factory at Rumonge, where Papa was supervisor at the time. He never left and now lived in the north of Bujumbura, in the district of Kamenge, with his wife and three sons. He always had biro lids peeping out of his pocket and, whenever he could, he read passages from the Bible that he kept tucked inside a crocodile-skin satchel. Every morning, Papa would give Donatien his instructions for the day and hand over a sum of money to pay the daily laborers.

The next person to make his entrance on the terrace was Innocent, who had come to collect the keys for Papa's pick-up truck. Innocent was a young Burundian, barely twenty years old. He was tall and thin, with a vertical scar running down his forehead that gave him a severe appearance he cultivated. A toothpick, already chewed on a thousand times, was forever wandering from one corner of his mouth to the other. He wore baggy trousers, a baseball cap, chunky white trainers, and a bracelet in the pan-African colors of red, green, and yellow. He was frequently in a foul mood and adopted a standoffish attitude toward the other employees, but Papa was very attached to him. Innocent was more than just the driver for Papa's business, he was a fixer. He knew Bujumbura inside out and had contacts everywhere: from the garage owners in Bwiza, the scrap-metal merchants in Buyenzi and the shopkeepers in the Asian quarter, to the soldiers in Camp Muha, the prostitutes in Kwijabe, and the meatball-sellers in the Central Market. . . . He knew whose palm to grease in order to unblock administrative requests that had been stuck for months on the desks of minor officials. The police never stopped him, and street kids watched over our pick-up for free.

Having communicated his instructions for the day, Papa poured the remains of the Thermos of tea into a pot containing a sad-leafed oleander, whistled two seconds of the "Marseillaise" to the parrot, and then we all jumped into the car.

7

THE FRENCH SCHOOL IN BUJUMBURA BROUGHT TO-
gether students of all ages, from *maternelle* through to *terminale*,
within its sprawling grounds. There were two main entrances:
the senior entrance, by the Prince Louis Rwagasore Stadium
and boulevard de l'Indépendence, leading directly to the office building, as well as the *collège* and *lycée* classrooms; and
the entrance for the infants, on the corner of avenue Muyinga
and boulevard de l'Uprona. In the middle was the *école pri-
maire*, which we attended. Force of habit meant that Papa still
dropped us off at the infants' entrance.

"Innocent will pick you up at midday and drive you to your
mother's shop. I'll be back tomorrow, I have to visit one of my
construction sites out of town."

"That's fine, Papa," said Ana sensibly.

"Gabriel, next Saturday you'll go with Innocent and Donatien to Cibitoke to sort out this bike business. You need to be
with them in order to identify it. Don't worry, we'll find your
bike."

THAT MORNING, the classroom was fizzing with excitement.
Our teacher had given each of us a letter, sent by a class of ten-
and eleven-year-old students, just like us, but from Orléans in

France. We couldn't wait to find out who our pen pals were. On the envelope in front of me, my name had been written in pink capital letters, surrounded by French flags, stars, and some hearts. The paper was sweetly perfumed. I unfolded the letter carefully. Inside, neat handwriting sloped to the left:

Friday 11th December 1992

Dear Gabriel,

My name is Laure and I am ten years old, just like you. I live in Orléans in a house with a garden. I'm tall with blond hair down to my shoulders, green eyes, and freckles. My little brother is called Mathieu. My dad is a doctor and my mum doesn't go to work. I like playing basketball and I know how to make crepes and bake biscuits. What about you?

I also like singing and dancing. What about you? I like watching TV. What about you? I don't like reading. What about you? When I grow up, I want to be a doctor like my dad. Every holiday, I stay with my cousins in the Vendée. Next year, I'm going to visit a new theme park called Disneyland. Do you know it? Can you send me your photo?

I can't wait to hear back from you.

Love,

Laure

PS: Did you get the rice we sent you?

Laure had enclosed her photo. She looked like one of Ana's dolls. I felt intimidated by her letter and I blushed when I read the word "love." It was as if I'd been sent a parcel of treats:

I was suddenly opening the doors to a mysterious world that I had never imagined existed. Laure from France, with her green eyes and blond hair, this girl who lived in a faraway place, was sending love to me, Gaby, from Kinanira. I was worried someone might notice my excitement, so I tucked her photo into a pocket of my schoolbag and put the letter back inside its envelope. I was already wondering which photo of me I could send her.

In the next lesson, the teacher asked each of us to write a letter in response to our pen pals.

Monday 4th January 1993

Dear Laure,

  My name is Gaby. Everything has a name, doesn't it? Roads, trees, insects . . . My neighborhood, for example, is Kinanira. My city is Bujumbura. My country is Burundi. My sister, mother and father, and my friends all have a name. A name they didn't choose. We're born with our name, and that's just how it is. One day, I asked my friends and family to call me Gaby instead of Gabriel, that way I could choose, rather than other people choosing for me. So please could you call me Gaby? I've got brown eyes, which means I only see people in brown. My mother, my father, my sister, Prothé, Donatien, Innocent, my friends . . . they've all got milk-with-coffee skin. Everyone sees the world through the color of their eyes. You've got green eyes, so I'd look green to you. I like lots of things I don't like. I like the sugar in ice-cream but not the cold. I like swimming pools but not the chlorine. I like school because of my friends and the atmosphere but I don't like the lessons. Grammar, subtraction, essays, punishments—they're so boring, it's barbaric! When

37

I grow up I want to be a mechanic, so nothing ever stays broken in my life. It's important to know how to fix things when they stop working. But all that's a long way off, I'm only ten and time drags sometimes, mainly in the afternoons when there's no school and on Sundays because there's nothing to do round at my grandmother's. Two months ago, the whole school had to be vaccinated against meningitis. It's a big deal if your brain gets sick, because you can't think anymore. So, in front of all the parents, the principal told us we had to have our injections, which I guess you'd expect him to say, what with our brains being his job and everything. This year, we're going to hold elections for the President of the Republic in Burundi. It's the first time it's happened. I won't be able to vote, I'll have to wait until I'm a mechanic. But I'll tell you the winner's name, I promise!

Bye for now.

Love,

Gaby

PS: I'll find out about the rice.

8

I SET OFF VERY EARLY WITH INNOCENT AND DONATIEN. The pick-up rattled along faster than usual, without any bags of concrete, or spades and pickaxes piled into the back. The three of us were embarking on a funny sort of adventure. Or that's what I was thinking as we approached the first military roadblock on the way out of Buja. What would we tell the soldiers if they stopped us? That we were on a dawn raid, headed for the other end of the country, to recover a stolen bicycle? We looked suspicious, no doubt about it. Innocent was at the wheel, chewing on the same old toothpick. It was a disgusting habit, in my view. All the wasters in Bujumbura had started doing it. Men who wanted to look tough and pass for cowboys, men like Innocent. I guess that one day, after watching a Clint Eastwood matinée at the Ciné Cameo, some poor guy figured he could stand out from the crowd, and in no time the trend spread through the city like wildfire. Two things travel fast in Bujumbura: rumors and trends.

Donatien had been slumped in a sulk from the start. He was sitting in the middle and couldn't find a comfortable position for his legs, because of the gearstick. He was all wonky, his left shoulder against Innocent's and his legs at an angle. I'd made a big fuss about wanting to be next to the window: it was raining and I liked following the trail of water droplets down the window, as well as blowing on the glass to draw in the condensation with my finger. It passed the time on long journeys through the countryside.

By the time we arrived in Cibitoke it had stopped raining. Donatien refused to let us drive up the track to the home of the twins' grandmother, because there was too much mud and we risked getting stuck. He suggested continuing by foot, but Innocent didn't want to get his white trainers dirty. So I went ahead with Donatien and we left Innocent in the truck, picking his stupid teeth.

Up in the hills, even when you think you're alone, there are always hundreds of pairs of eyes watching you, and your presence is announced for kilometers around by voices that ricochet from one hut—or *rugo*—to another. So, by the time we reached the old woman she was already waiting for us and holding two glasses of milk curds. Donatien and I couldn't speak much Kirundi, especially not the complex and poetic Kirundi of the hills, which required more than a few words of Swahili or French to plug the gaping holes in our vocabulary. I'd never really learned Kirundi, because everybody spoke French in Buja. Donatien was from Kivu in Zaire, and the Zaireans from Kivu often speak only Swahili or classic Sorbonne-style French.

Here, it was a very different story. In the interior of the country, it's impossible to have a conversation with people like the twins' grandmother: there are too many subtleties in their language, with its references to proverbs from time immemorial and expressions that date back to the Stone Age. Donatien and I were not at that level. Still, the old woman tried explaining where we could find the bicycle's new owner. Having failed to understand a single word she had spoken, we made our way back down to the car with Godefroy and Balthazar, the twins' famous willy-snipping cousins, to find Innocent, who would have to act as our translator. We hit the road again, with the cousins in the back of the pick-up ready to show us the way. Two kilometers out of town, another track led us to a village where we found a boy called Mathias, the one who'd been spotted by the twins riding my bike. It turned out that this Mathias had sold it on to a certain Stanislas, from Gihomba. So we climbed back into the pick-up, along with the two cousins plus Mathias, to track down the famous Stanislas, who, it transpired, had in turn sold the bike to a beekeeper in Kurigitari. Off we set again, this time bound for Kurigitari and with Stanislas on board. It was the same story with the beekeeper, who joined us to help with the address of the new owner, a man from Gitaba, by the name of Jean-Bosco. Once in Gitaba, we were informed that Jean-Bosco was in Cibitoke. So back we went to Cibitoke. And there, Jean-Bosco explained that he had just sold the bike to a farmer from Gitaba . . .

About-turn. Except that, as we were driving along the main road out of Cibitoke, we got stopped by the police who enquired what we were up to, with nine of us piled into one vehicle. Innocent started telling the story of the stolen bike and the hunt for its new owner. It was midday and curious passersby were quick to rush over. In no time, hundreds of people had surrounded the pick-up.

Opposite us was the central *cabaret*, which did the biggest trade in drinks in town. The mayor and a few local bigwigs were polishing off a serving of goat-meat skewers washed down with bottles of warm Primus. The crowd that had gathered around us swiftly attracted their attention. The mayor stood up gingerly from his stool. He burped, hoisted up his trousers, adjusted his belt, and headed in our direction like a weary chameleon, slicing through the crowd with his big belly, greasy chops, and a greenish-yellow shirt covered in meat stains. His face was long and thin, but his fat auntie's backside extended right up the middle of his back, and his paunch was as taut and stretched as that of a pregnant woman at full term. He looked like a calabash, this mayor.

While the rabble argued among itself, I suddenly spotted Calixte in the crowd. The same Calixte who had stolen my bike. No sooner had I sounded the alert than he scarpered faster than a green mamba. The entire town ran after him, as if chasing a chicken whose neck needed wringing in time for lunch. There's nothing like a spot of blood sport during the midday lull to kill time in the sleepy provinces. Popular justice is the name they give to lynching, it has the benefit of sounding civilized. Luckily, the crowd didn't have the last word that day. They caught Calixte, but the police swiftly intercepted the democratic thrashing. At which point the mayor attempted to gain the upper hand by playing the wise man intent on calming heated spirits, with a pompous speech about the importance of being an honest citizen. But his flights of lyricism fell flat, at that hour and in that swelter. He gave up mid-speech and returned to his proper place, in front of a beer, to calm his own spirit. Calixte, who was in a terrible mess, was remanded in custody while Donatien rushed off to press charges.

Putting Calixte behind bars didn't fix the problem of my bike, so we decided to look up the beekeeper from Gitaba. This meant, once again, following the track that led to the twins' grandmother's house and then continuing farther. Innocent insisted on taking matters into his own hands and driving the pick-up through the mud, despite Donatien's insistent warnings about getting stuck. In the locality of Gitaba there was a small clay house with a roof covered in banana-tree leaves. The hut was at the top of a hill, where we were captivated by the view that suddenly revealed itself. Rain had washed the sky, while the rays of sunshine striking the sodden ground traced spirals of pinkish mist above a vast green plain intersected by the ocher waters of the Rusizi river. Donatien admired the spectacle with religious awe, while Innocent, who couldn't have cared less, removed the grime from under his fingernails with the same revolting toothpick that had been in his mouth moments earlier. The beauty of the world wasn't his concern, he was only interested in the filth from his own body.

In the yard, a woman was kneeling on a mat grinding sorghum into flour. Behind her, a man perched on a stool invited us over. He was the farmer. At home, when a stranger turned up, even before saying hello, Papa would bark irritably: "What d'you want?" Here it was the opposite, there was restraint and politeness. We didn't feel like strangers. No matter that we'd appeared unannounced in these people's small yard, tucked away on a mountaintop, they gave us the reassuring impression that they'd been expecting us for a long time. Before enquiring as to the reason for our visit, the farmer invited us to be seated. He had just returned from the fields. His bare feet were covered in dry mud, his shirt patched and his cotton trousers rolled up at the knees. Behind him, an earth-clogged hoe was propped against the hut wall. A girl brought us three chairs, while the woman smiled and carried on grinding the grain between two stones.

We had barely sat down when a boy of my age pedaled at high speed into the yard on my bike. Without stopping to think, I leaped from my chair and flung myself at the handlebars. The family stood up in bewilderment, casting distraught looks in our direction. The boy was too surprised to resist as I wrenched the bike out of his hands. There was a very awkward pause and Donatien shook Innocent's shoulder, urging him to speak in Kirundi and explain the reason for our visit. Innocent exerted a superhuman effort to stir himself from his seat, where he had already made himself comfortable. He seemed unenthusiastic about repeating the same explanations he'd given earlier to the police, but eventually he told the whole story, right from the beginning, in a flat monotone. The family listened in silence. The boy's face crumpled as the situation gradually dawned on him. When Innocent had finished, the farmer began to explain in turn, tilting his head to the left and opening the palms of his hands to the sky, as if imploring us to spare his life. He said that he had made sacrifices in order to give his son this present, that he had saved up for a long time, that they were people of modest means and good Christians. Innocent didn't appear to be listening: he scratched the inside of his ear with his toothpick, before inspecting the gunge on the tip with keen interest. Donatien was embarrassed that our hosts clearly felt so confused and dismayed, but he didn't dare say anything. While the farmer was still talking, Innocent walked toward me, grabbed the bike, and loaded it into the back of the pick-up. His irritation was apparent as he coldly advised the family to confront the person responsible for their misfortune, currently to be found in prison in Cibitoke. He pointed out that all they had to do was press charges against Calixte in order to get their money back. Then he signaled to me to climb into the pick-up. Donatien joined us reluctantly. I could see that his mind was racing for a solution. He took a deep breath as he sat down next to me in the front.

"Gabriel, for pity's sake, let's not take the bike. What we're doing is worse than stealing. We're breaking a child's heart."

"That's all?" jibed Innocent.

"What about me?" I wanted to know. "My heart was broken when Calixte stole my bike."

"Of course it was, but the bike doesn't mean as much to you

as it does to this boy," Donatien continued. "He's very poor and his father worked so hard to give him this present. If we leave with the bike, he'll never own another one again."

"What are you playing at?" Innocent shot Donatien a nasty look. "D' you think you're Robin Hood or something? Just because they're a poor family, are we supposed to hand over what doesn't belong to them?"

"Innocent, you and I grew up in this kind of poverty. We both know they'll never get their money back, which means they'll have lost years' worth of savings through no fault of their own. You understand how it goes, my friend."

"I'm not your friend! And here's my advice: stop feeling sorry for these people. They're all cheats and liars in backward places like this."

"Gabriel," said Donatien, turning to face me again, "we could tell the boss we didn't manage to find your bike, and then he'll buy you another one. It'll be our little secret, for which God will forgive us, because it's in the name of doing good. To help a poor child."

"So your plan is to lie?" asked Innocent. "I thought your precious God was against that kind of thing? Leave Gabriel out of it, stop blaming him. Anyway, the other kid lives on a bloody farm, what's he going to do with a BMX? Let's go!"

I couldn't bring myself to turn around or look in the rearview mirror. Our mission was accomplished. We had found my bike. The rest was none of my business, or that's what Innocent said.

When we got stuck in the mud a few minutes later, just as Donatien had predicted we would, he recited a passage from the Bible that spoke about difficult times, selfish men, the end of days, and then he began muttering all sorts of things under his breath that frightened me. He took it as a sign that God was punishing us for our bad deed. I pretended to be asleep for the entire journey, to avoid meeting his eye. However much I tried to justify what we'd done, I felt a mounting sense of shame. When we arrived back at the house, I told Innocent and Donatien that I would never touch the bike again, to make amends for my behavior. Staring at me with a mixture of exasperation and disbelief, Innocent muttered, "Spoiled brat," and headed off to the kiosk to buy a new packet of toothpicks. Donatien leaned over me, his big square head a few centimeters from my face, his bitter breath hinting at an empty, acidic stomach. His eyes brimmed with an icy anger that cut me to the core.

"The damage is done, kid," he spelled out slowly.

9

MY GRANDMOTHER LIVED IN A SMALL HOUSE WITH green rendered walls, in a settlement administered by the Office of African Municipalities (OCAF), in Ngagara, District 2, Bujumbura. Mamie shared the house with her mother, who was my great-grandmother Rosalie, as well as Mamie's son, my uncle Pacifique, studying in his final year at the lycée Saint-Albert. Pacifique was a seriously good-looking guy. Every girl in the neighborhood was after him. But his only loves were his comic books, his guitar, and singing. His voice wasn't as exceptional as Maman's, but he was an outstanding performer. He worshipped the French crooners we heard constantly on the radio, singing about love, or sadness, or sadness in love. His renditions of their songs made them his own. As he closed his eyes, screwed up his face and began to weep, the whole family fell quiet, even old Rosalie who didn't understand a word of French. We listened without moving, or if we did, it was just the tips of our ears that wiggled, like the hippopotamuses floating in the port.

For the most part, Mamie's neighbors were Rwandans who had left their country to escape carnage, massacres, wars, pogroms, purges, destruction, fires, tsetse flies, pillaging, apartheid, rapes, murders, settling of scores, and I don't know what else. Like Maman and her family, they had fled those problems only to encounter new ones in Burundi—poverty, exclusion, quotas, xenophobia, rejection, being made into scapegoats, depression, homesickness, and nostalgia. The problems of refugees.

War had broken out in Rwanda two years ago, when I turned eight. It happened at the beginning of the school year. We heard on Radio France Internationale that the rebels—Rwandan refugees who had joined from the bordering countries of Uganda, Burundi, and Zaire—had launched a surprise attack. Their army, the Rwandan Patriotic Front, was on the move. Maman danced and sang when she heard this news. I had never seen her so elated.

But her happiness had been short-lived. A few days later we had received news of the death of Alphonse. Alphonse was Maman's other brother, the oldest in the family and Mamie's pride and joy. He was a brilliant man: a chemical engineer awarded degrees from the most prestigious universities in Europe and America. It was Alphonse who had coached me in maths and planted in my head the idea of becoming a mechanic. Papa was very fond of him and used to say: "If we had ten men like Alphonse, Burundi would become the next Singapore in no time." Alphonse had been top of the class, but he was also as laid-back as the class joker. He was always having fun, joking around, tickling us under the arms and kissing Maman on the neck to embarrass her. And when he laughed, happiness washed over the walls of Mamie's small living room like a fresh lick of paint.

Alphonse had left for the front without telling anyone, or leaving a note behind. The RPF didn't care about his diplomas. As far as they were concerned, he was just another soldier. He died there, one of the brave, for a country he didn't know, where he had never set foot before. He died there, in the mud, killed in action in a cassava field, like some soldier who didn't know his two times table, let alone how to read or write.

When he'd had too much to drink, Alphonse suffered from the same melancholy that afflicts all children of exiles. One day, as if experiencing a premonition, he had spoken about his own funeral. He said he wanted a big party with clowns and jugglers and people wearing colorful *pagnes*—wrap-skirts and other outfits in the wax-print cotton you could buy at the Central Market—and fire-eaters and sun eulogies, without a depressing requiem or a Nunc Dimittis or a gloomy face in sight. On the day of Tonton Alphonse's funeral, Pacifique took his guitar along and sang his favorite song for his older brother. It told the story of a former soldier denouncing the absurdity of war. It was a song that could have been written about Alphonse: funny on the surface but sad deep down. Pacifique's voice gave out before he made it to the end.

AND NOW, two years later, in early January '93, it was Pacifique who had made up his mind to set off for war. He had already talked about it with Mamie. So on this particular Sunday morning, once we were back from Mass and sitting round the table, Maman didn't hold back.

"We're worried about you, Pacifique. Your teacher, Mr. Kimenyi, has been in touch with Mamie. It seems you're not attending your classes at Saint-Albert anymore?"

"All the other Rwandan students in my year have gone to the front. And I'm getting ready too, big sister!"

"You should wait. The peace agreements will bear fruit. I was over at Aunt Eusébie's in Kigali ten days ago, and they are hopeful, they believe matters can be resolved through political channels. So just be patient, please!"

"I don't have any faith in the extremists. The Rwandan government is keen to throw the international community off the scent, but in the interior of the country the militia continues to be armed, the media is being used to incite violence, and massacres and targeted killings are being carried out. Politicians give hate-fueled speeches, calling on the people to hunt us down and throw us into the Nyabarongo river. So it's up to us to organize ourselves in response. We have to be ready to fight back if the peace agreements fail. This is about our survival, big sister."

Neither Mamie nor Rosalie said anything. Maman's eyes were closed as she rubbed her temples. The neighbors' radio was broadcasting hymns. We could hear forks clinking against plates. A gentle breeze raised the curtain at the window. In the heat, a fine layer of sweat glistened on Pacifique's handsome skin. His jaw muscles were tense from the piece of beef he was chewing on, and I sensed that the unspoken subject at table— the death of Alphonse—was as present as the flies Ana kept fishing out of the tomato sauce.

After lunch, Mamie ordered everybody to go and lie down, as usual. I went off to have my siesta in Pacifique's bedroom, which used to be Maman's room when she was a girl. There was no window, just two camp beds on either side of the tiny room and, hanging from a bare flex, a light bulb painted red that cast a sinister light over green walls covered in posters. Pacifique slept on the bedstead springs, he said it was to get used to the tough conditions of life at the front. In the mornings, he rose early to train on the beach with a small group of young Rwandan men. They ran on sand along the shore of Lake Tanganyika. Some days they only ate a handful of beans, in preparation for hunger and hardship.

Lying on the bed, I recalled the face of the boy I had

reclaimed my bike from the day before, as well as Donatien's lecture about God's work, selflessness, making sacrifices, and the rest of the horrendous guilt trip. Since yesterday I'd been feeling vain, selfish, and generally ashamed of the whole episode: I had gone from victim to executioner, simply by wishing to retrieve something that belonged to me in the first place. I needed to talk to someone about it, to banish my dark thoughts.

"Pacifique," I whispered, "are you asleep?"

"Mmm . . ."

"D'you believe in God?"

"What?"

"D'you believe in God?"

"No, I'm a communist. I believe in the people. Now leave me alone!"

"Who's that on the calendar, above your bed?"

"Fred Rwigema, commander of the RPF. He's a hero. It's thanks to him we're fighting. He gave us back our sense of pride."

"So are you going to fight by his side?"

"He died. At the beginning of our campaign."

"Oh . . . Who killed him?"

"You ask too many questions, kid. Get some sleep!"

There was the creaking of metal as Pacifique turned over to face the wall. I could never nap during siesta-time, or see the point in it. The night was enough to restore my energy. So I waited for the minutes to pass. I was only allowed to get up if I heard a grown-up walking about in the house. I interrogated every noise, listening out for the first movement that might signal my release from the mattress. Sometimes I had to wait for two hours. The door onto the living room was ajar, allowing a small amount of light to seep in. I examined the posters on the walls. They were pages from magazines, crudely stuck up using

51

wallpaper paste. The stars of Maman's youth rubbed shoulders with those of Pacifique's: France Gall between Michael Jackson and Jean-Pierre Papin; a photo of Pope Jean-Paul II visiting Burundi encroaching on one of Tina Turner's legs and Jimi Hendrix's guitar; a Kenyan toothpaste advert covering a poster of James Dean. To kill time, I scooped up Pacifique's pile of comics from under the bed: *Alain Chevallier, Spirou* magazine, *Tintin, Rahan* . . .

As soon as the household began to stir, I leaped out of bed to keep Rosalie company. Every afternoon, she observed the same ritual. She would make herself comfortable on a mat in the backyard, open her snuffbox crafted from vegetable ivory, stuff pinches of tobacco into her wooden pipe, then light a match and, eyes closed, take the first small tokes of fresh tobacco. Next, she would remove some sisal fibers or banana-tree leaves from a plastic bag and weave them into coasters and conical baskets. She sold her handiwork in the town center in order to contribute to the household finances, which survived thanks to Mamie's small nurse's salary and sporadic handouts from Maman.

Rosalie's frizzy gray-white hair stood on end like a chef's toque perched on top of her head. It made her skull appear oblong-shaped and disproportionately large for the graceful neck supporting it: like a rugby ball balanced on a needle. Rosalie was nearly a hundred years old. She often liked to tell the life-story of this or that king who had rebelled first against the German and then the Belgian colonists, and who had been exiled abroad for refusing to convert to Christianity. I never showed much interest in the antics of the monarchy and the White Fathers. I always yawned, which irritated Pacifique, who scolded me for my lack of curiosity. Maman would fire back that her children were French kids, and it was pointless boring us with their Rwandan stories. Pacifique, on the other hand, could spend hours listening to the old woman recalling the Rwanda of bygone days: heroic deeds in battle, pastoral poetry, panegyric poems, the Intore dances, the genealogy of the clans, moral values . . .

Mamie berated Maman for not speaking to us in Kinyarwanda. She believed that the language would allow us to hold onto our identity, despite living in exile, otherwise we would never become good Banyarwandas ("those who come from Rwanda"). Maman didn't buy those arguments: in her eyes we were white kids, with skin the color of pale caramel, but white all the same. Whenever we spoke a few words of Kinyarwanda, she immediately made fun of our accent. So it's hardly surprising I showed little interest in Rwanda, its monarchy, its cows, its mountains, its moons, its milk, its honey, and its rotten mead.

As these afternoons drew to a close, Rosalie continued to recount the stories of her era, her sepia memories of an idealized Rwanda. She would insist that she didn't want to die in exile like King Musinga. That it was important for her to breathe her last on home soil, in the land of her ancestors. Rosalie would speak slowly and softly in a gentle murmur, with the cadences of a sitar player. Her cataracts made her eyes appear blue. A tear or two was always poised to slide down one cheek.

Pacifique liked to soak up the old woman's words. He would nod while being lulled by his grandmother's nostalgia. But on this particular evening he clasped those tiny hands of hers, flat and bony, between his own, and whispered that the persecution was soon going to stop, that it was time for them to go back home, that Burundi wasn't their country and they weren't meant to stay refugees forever. The old woman was clinging to her past, to her lost homeland, while the young man was peddling her a future, a new and modern country for all Rwandans, regardless of their identity. And yet they were both talking about the same thing. Returning to their country. One belonged to history, the other was tasked with making history happen.

A warm wind enveloped us, wrapping itself fleetingly around us before taking off again into the distance, carrying with it precious promises. In the sky, the first stars began to flicker shyly. They shone down on Mamie's small yard, far below on earth, a square of exile where my family traded the dreams and hopes that life seemed to impose on them.

10

IT WAS GINO'S IDEA, TO START WITH. HE WANTED us to find a name for our band of brothers. We kept going round in circles. We thought of The Three Musketeers, but there were five of us. The twins' suggestions were all cringeworthy, along the lines of "The Five Fingers" or "The Best Friends in the World." Gino thought we should give ourselves an American name. Anything American was in at school, everybody said "cool" all the time, they swaggered or snake-walked, had designs shaved into their scalp, and played basketball in baggy clothes. But Gino's main inspiration came from the American R&B group Boyz II Men that we used to watch on the music show *Au-delà du Son* on Saturday-night TV. We thought it could work, because there was a Burundian in the group, so it would be a tribute to him. We didn't know for sure, but in Bujumbura the rumor was that the tall, skinny guy in Boyz II Men came from Bwiza or Nyakabiga, not that any journalist had ever confirmed this. Another reason for Gino wanting us to be called Kinanira Boyz was to stamp our mark as the new kings of the street, to make it clear that we controlled the neighborhood and nobody else could impose their law.

The *impasse*—the cul-de-sac where all five of us lived—was the zone we knew best. It was some two hundred meters long, a dirt and stone track with avocado trees and spider flowers

55

growing down the middle of it, which naturally formed a road with two lanes. The gaps in the bougainvillea hedges afforded glimpses of elegant houses set in gardens planted with fruit trees and palm trees. The lemongrass bordering the gutter gave off a gentle perfume that kept the mosquitoes at bay.

The twins' house was opposite mine, at the entrance, first on the left. They were mixed race too, with a French father and a Burundian mother. Their parents owned a video rental shop, specializing in U.S. comedies and Bollywood films. On afternoons when it was pouring with rain, we would all go over to their house and hang out in front of the telly. Sometimes, on the sly, we even watched sex movies for grown-ups, but we weren't so keen on them, apart from Armand, who stared at the screen with his eyes popping out of his head while rubbing himself against a cushion, like a dog on someone's leg.

Armand lived in the big white-brick house at the end of our street. Both his parents were Burundian, making him the only black kid in our group. His father was a thickset man with sideburns so long they joined up with his mustache to form a circle around his eyes and nose. He worked as a diplomat in the Middle East and knew many heads of state personally. Armand had a photo pinned above his bed from when he was a baby, in a romper suit, on the knees of Colonel Gaddafi. Because his father was always traveling, Armand lived for most of the time with just his mother and big sisters: they were all sour and sanctimonious, and I'd never seen them smile. Despite everyone being so strict and uptight in his family, Armand had decided that his role was to dance about and play the clown. He lived in fear of his father, who only returned from his travels to exert his authority over his children. No hugs, no displays of affection. Ever. He would deliver a slap in the face and then hop on a plane bound for Tripoli or Carthage. Consequently,

Armand had two personalities: one at home and one in the street. Heads or tails.

And then there was Gino. The oldest kid in the group, by a year and nine months. He had stayed down a year at school on purpose, to be in the same class as us. Or at least that was his excuse for not making his grades. He lived with his father in an old colonial house, behind the big red gate in the middle of our street. His father was Belgian and a lecturer in political science at the University of Bujumbura. His mother was Rwandan, like Maman, but none of us had ever seen her. Sometimes Gino told us she was working in Kigali, sometimes she was in Europe.

We spent our days arguing the way friends do, but it goes without saying that we loved each other like brothers. In the afternoons, once lunch was over, the five of us would slope off to our headquarters: the carcass of a Volkswagen Combi on a patch of wasteland. We laughed and had heated debates inside that van, smoked Supermatch cigarettes in secret, listened to Gino's incredible stories as well as the twins' jokes, and Armand performed astounding feats: revealing the underneath of his eyelids by flipping them inside out, touching his nose with his tongue, twisting his thumb backward until it met his arm, using his front teeth to take the tops off bottles, or chewing on *pili-pili* hot peppers and swallowing them without wincing. It was in that VW Combi that we plotted our futures, from small outings to grand excursions. We were full of dreams and it was with impatient hearts that we imagined the joys and adventures life held in store for us. In short, we felt at one with the world, in our hideout on the patch of wasteland by our street.

One afternoon, we were roaming the neighborhood in search of mangoes. We had given up on our old technique of throwing stones to dislodge the fruit from their branches on the day Armand had hurled a stone a bit too far and damaged his father's Mercedes. His old man had given him a beating to remember. Armand's screams rang out all the way from the closed-off end of our street to the Rumonge road, as his father's wide belt sliced through the air. After that episode, we rigged up long poles with wire hooks on the end, held together with old bicycle tubes. These rods were over six meters long, allowing us to pick off even the most inaccessible mangoes.

A few drivers shouted insults as we traipsed along the main road, because they didn't like the look of us. Barefoot and bare-chested, with our rods scraping the ground and our T-shirts tied in bundles around the mangoes we'd harvested, we were a sight to behold.

A smartly dressed woman, who was probably a friend of Armand's parents, walked past. When she recognized Armand, with his exposed torso and his feet covered in dust, she glanced skyward and made the sign of the cross: "Dear God! Put your clothes back on quickly, my child. You look like a street urchin." Grown-ups cracked us up, sometimes.

Back on home turf, we had our eyes on the big, fat juicy mangoes hanging in the Von Gotzens' garden. We'd managed to hook a few from the street side with our rods, but the most mouthwatering were out of reach. We'd have needed to climb the low wall, but we were frightened of encountering Monsieur Von Gotzen, an old German who was a little crazy: he was a crossbow collector who had done time in prison, once for urinating in his gardener's food—the latter having dared to ask for a pay rise—and then for locking his houseboy in the freezer as a punishment for burning the banana flambés to a crisp. His wife, who was more discreet but also more racist, played golf every day in the grounds of the Méridien Hotel and was the president of the Bujumbura equestrian club, where she spent most of her days pampering her horse, a handsome thorough-bred with a lustrous black coat. Their house was the grandest on our street, and the only one with an upstairs and a pool, but we steered clear of them.

Opposite, behind the twins' place, was the house that belonged to Madame Economopoulos, an old Greek lady with no children and ten dachshunds. We managed to sneak under her fence, thanks to a hole dug by the neighborhood dogs for nocturnal visits when the female dachshunds were in heat. In her shaded garden, as well as the giant mango tree there were vines covered with fruit, probably the only vines in the entire country, and an abundance of flowers.

Armand and I were pilfering bunches of grapes while Gino and the twins picked off the fleshiest mangoes, when the Greek woman's houseboy arrived on the scene in a fury, brandishing a broom above his head. He opened the dogs' enclosure, and the dachshunds immediately gave chase. We were out of there quick as a flash, sneaking back under the fencing. In our scramble, Armand ripped his shorts when they snagged on the barbed wire. He had us in fits of laughter for a good quarter of an hour, with his bare patch of buttock. After that, we stationed ourselves in front of Madame Economopoulos's gates. We knew that she returned home from the town center at the same time every day, and that she'd be glad to see us.

When she appeared, in her small red Lada, we rushed over to the car door to sell her our mangoes. Or, strictly speaking, *her* mangoes. She bought ten or so from us, before her houseboy opened the gates and we bolted with a one-thousand-franc note in our pocket. The houseboy was beside himself, hurling his broom into the air and calling us all sorts of names in Kirundi, but we were already long gone.

With the remains of our crop, we returned to the Combi

to gorge ourselves in an orgy of mangoes. Juice flowed down our chins, our cheeks, our arms, our clothes, and our feet. The slippery stones were sucked, sheared and shaved, while the underside of the skin was scraped and cleared out, then cleaned again. The stringy flesh clung between our teeth.

Once we were sated and inebriated from all that juice and fruit pulp, short of breath and round of belly, the five of us flopped onto the dusty old Combi seats, heads lolling backward. Our hands were sticky and our nails black, our smiles broad and our hearts sugary. Ours was the well-earned rest of the mango-pickers.

"Why don't we mess around in the Muha?" suggested Armand.

"Nah, not the river, I'd rather go fishing at the sailing club!" said Gino.

"How about a game of football on the pitch at the International School?" the twins joined in.

"We could head over to the Swiss guy's place to play Atari?" I said.

"Forget about it, he's an idiot, that piece of cheese-with-holes-in! He charges five hundred francs for a round of Pac-Man!"

We ended up walking down the river Muha, all the way to the sailing club. It was a proper expedition. At one point, we stumbled upon a waterfall that nearly swept the twins away. The rainy season had made the current stronger. In front of the sailing club, we made fishing rods from bamboo reeds and bought maggots and flour as bait. The Omani seller from the Asian neighborhood was always down on the beach. People called him Ninja because he spent his days performing karate moves in thin air while shouting, as if he were fighting thousands of invisible enemies. Grown-ups said he was crazy, with his martial-arts obsession. But the children were fond of him: we reckoned what he did was a lot more normal than plenty of other grown-up stuff, like organizing military parades, spraying deodorant under their arms, wearing ties in hot weather, sitting in the dark drinking beer all night, and listening to Zairean rumbas that never seemed to end.

WE SAT down on the riverbank, in front of the sailing-club restaurant, a few meters from a pod of frolicking hippopotamuses. There was a strong wind, the lake was flecked with the white crests of waves, and the spray at the foot of the rocks looked like soapy foam. Gino started peeing in the water. He wanted us to have a who-can-pee-farthest competition, but nobody was in the mood. The twins had barely recovered from being circumcized, Armand was shy about that part of his anatomy, and when I saw that the others weren't joining in, I bailed out.

"You bunch of wimps, you chicken shits, you lumps of rotten goat's meat!"

"Up yours, Gino, go ahead and piss as far as Zaire, and then Mobutu can send the BSP to cut your balls off."

"It's Francis's balls I'm going to cut off, if I keep seeing him hanging around our area," Gino replied, still peeing as far as possible.

"Here we go! It's been a while since you mentioned his name. You'd better watch out, or we'll think you've got a crush on him."

"Kinanira is ours! I'm going to beat the shit out of that son-of-a-you-know-what!" Gino shouted, leaning into the wind and opening his arms wide.

"Stop showing off, we all know you won't do anything to

him. Your mouth is so full of shit, you're like a crocodile from the Ganges!"

Francis was old in our eyes, about thirteen or fourteen. He was the bitter enemy of Gino and our crew. The trouble was, Francis was stronger than all five of us put together. Not that he looked particularly solid; far from it, he was all wiry. Dry as deadwood. But to us he seemed invincible. His arms and legs were like lianas covered with scars and burns. It was as if he had metal plates under his skin in some places, preventing him from experiencing any pain. One day, he cornered Armand because he wanted to extort the Jojo chewing gum we'd just bought from the kiosk. I gave him one hell of a kick in the shin to make my getaway, and he didn't even wince. I was speechless.

Francis lived with an elderly uncle, opposite the Muha bridge, just one and a half streets away, in a gloomy house covered in lichen. The river flowed past the bottom of his garden, thick and brown like an African rock python. We used to hide in the ditch when we went past his house. He hated us with a vengeance, calling us rich kids and spoiled brats with afternoon tea at four o'clock. This drove Gino mad, what with his dreams of becoming the boss of Bujumbura. Francis claimed to be a former *mayibobo*, a street kid, with first-hand knowledge of the gangs from Ngagara and Bwiza, the ones people called "The Invincibles" and "The Diehards," and which had featured in the newspapers for a while now because they fleeced honest citizens.

I didn't dare admit to the others that I was scared of Francis. I wasn't keen when Gino insisted on fights and fisticuffs to protect our street, because I could see my friends becoming increasingly fired up by what he said. Not that I wasn't roused too, but I preferred it when we made dugouts from the trunks of banana trees to travel down the Muha, or watched birds through binoculars in the maize fields behind the International School, or built tree houses in the local rubber fig trees and acted out endless cowboys and Indians adventures. We knew all the hiding places in our cul-de-sac, and we wanted to stay there for the rest of our lives, all five of us, together.

No MATTER how hard I try, I can't pinpoint the moment when we began to think differently. To believe that, from then on, we would be on one side, with our enemies like Francis on the other. I've raided my memories, but I can't recall exactly when it was that we decided it was no longer enough to share the little we had and that instead we would stop trusting, that we would see other people as a threat and erect an invisible barrier against the outside world by transforming our neighborhood into a fortress and our street into a sealed-off area.

I still wonder when it was that our little gang began to feel scared.

11

NOTHING IS SWEETER THAN THE MOMENT WHEN THE sun sinks behind the ridge of the mountains. Dusk brings with it the cool of evening and warm colors that deepen with every minute. This is the hour that marks a change in rhythm. People head home from work at a leisurely pace, the night watchmen come on duty, and neighbors sit out in front of their gates. There is silence before the toads and crickets start up. Often, it's the perfect time for a game of football, for sitting with a friend on the low wall above the gutter, for gluing your ear to the radio, or for visiting a neighbor.

With the tedium of the afternoon finally ebbing away, it would be in that interval, in those slow-moving minutes, that I would find Gino in front of his garage, beneath the scented frangipani tree, and the two of us would lie down on the mat belonging to the *zamu* or night watchman. He would let us tune into news from the front line on his small crackling radio set. Gino would fiddle with the aerial to reduce the hissing. He translated every sentence for me, putting his whole heart into it.

The war in Rwanda had resumed a few days earlier. Pacifique had picked up his kit bag and left his guitar behind. The Rwandan Patriotic Front was on its way to liberate us, Gino declared. He cursed the fact that he was stuck here unable to do anything: as far as he was concerned, we were cowards, our

64

job was to go and fight. There were rumors of mixed-race kids like us joining up. Gino even claimed that some of them were Kadogos, child soldiers of twelve or thirteen.

Gino, my best friend, who was scared of the trapdoor spiders we collected in his garden and who flattened himself to the ground whenever we heard a thunderstorm rumbling in the distance, this same Gino wanted to wage guerrilla warfare, with a Kalashnikov bigger than he was, in the mist of the Virunga mountains. He had scratched his skin with a branch until he drew blood, tattooing "RPF" into his forearm. His skin had scarred badly, leaving three swollen letters. He was half-Rwandan like me, but secretly I envied him because he spoke fluent Kinyarwanda and knew exactly who he was. It got on Papa's nerves, seeing a twelve-year-old joining in adult conversations. But there were no secrets when it came to politics, as far as Gino was concerned. His father was a university lecturer and he always asked for Gino's opinion on the news, recommending that he read this article in *Jeune Afrique* or that one in *Le Soir*. Which meant that Gino always understood everything grown-ups said. This was also his handicap.

Gino, the only boy I knew who drank black coffee with no sugar for breakfast, while listening to the news on Radio France Internationale with the same enthusiasm that I reserved for a Vital'O football match. When we were together, he insisted on me acquiring what he called an "identity." According to him, there was a certain way of being, of feeling and thinking, that I should adopt. His words echoed Maman's and Pacifique's and he kept repeating that we were just refugees here in Burundi and we had to return to our home, to Rwanda.

My home? But that was here. Yes, I was the son of a Rwandan woman, but my reality was Burundi, the French school, Kinanira, our street. Nothing else existed. Still, with the death of Alphonse, and now Pacifique's departure, there were times when I felt as if politics did affect me. I was afraid, though. Afraid of how Papa would react if he heard me talking about these things. Afraid because I didn't want to introduce chaos into my neatly ordered world, for this was about war and, in my mind, that could only mean sadness and misfortune.

That evening, we were listening to the radio when nightfall caught us unawares. We withdrew into the house, where the walls of Gino's living room displayed a gallery of animal portraits. His father was an avid photographer. At weekends, he would set off in his uniform of hat, short-sleeved shirt, capitula shorts, light sandals, and socks to go on photo-safari in the Ruvubu Natural Park. Then he would lock himself away in the blacked-out bathroom to develop his negatives. Gino's house had the whiff of a dental surgery about it, the pong of chemicals from the photo lab mingling with the eau de toilette his father splashed on liberally. He was like a ghost, Gino's old man. We hardly ever saw him, but you could tell he was around thanks to the pervasive smell of bleached toilets that clung to his skin, and the rattle of the typewriter on which he spent his life hammering out lectures and political books. Gino's father liked cleanliness and order. After any simple task, such as opening the curtains or watering the plants, he would say: "Right, that's done!" The whole stupid day long he would tick off in his head whatever he had accomplished, muttering: "That's one more thing done!" He brushed the hairs on his forearm so they all lay in the same direction. He had a bald patch at the back of his head, which he disguised with a comb-over. On days when he wore a normal tie, he would comb over from the right; on days when he wore a bow-tie, the comb-over was from the left. He was meticulous about trimming the hairs around his sunroof, always leaving a narrow strip of bald patch exposed, like an uncamouflaged trench on his head. Despite his passion for photography, his nickname in the neighborhood was Kojak not Kodak, because of his spreading bald patch.

When he was at home, Gino wasn't much fun to be around—he was less into messing about and spitting and burping and wedging my head between his buttocks while breaking wind. He followed me about like an infatuated poodle, checking to see if I'd flushed, if I'd left any drops on the toilet seat, if I'd put the knick-knacks back where they belonged in the living room. Not only did his father's fussiness infect him, but it made the house seem cold and unfriendly.

Despite the warm tropical night, even Gino could sense the polar wind blasting through those rooms. After a few minutes we looked one another in the eye, sensing that neither of us felt comfortable round at his place. Without a word, we walked away from the dingy neon lighting, leaving the moths to be gobbled up by the geckos, heading out of earshot of the maddening clickety-clack of his father's Olivetti and back out into the reassuring darkness.

When the two of us strolled along our street, we would hold hands and tell each other what was happening in our lives. Gino was the only friend I felt comfortable enough with to overcome my shyness and confide in from time to time. After my parents' separation, I had been pondering some new questions.

"Do you miss your mother?"

"I'll see her soon. She's in Kigali."

"Didn't you tell me she was in Europe, last time?"

"Yes, but she's back now."

"Are your parents separated?"

"No, not really. It's just that they don't live together."

"Don't they love each other anymore?"

"Of course they do! Why d'you ask?"

67

"Because they don't live together. Isn't that what it's like when parents don't love each other anymore?"

"That's what it's like for you, Gaby, not me . . ."

Slowly, we drew closer to the pale glow of the storm lantern hanging from the kiosk. In front of the shipping container-cum-grocery store, I took out what remained of the thousand francs Madame Economopoulos had given us. We bought a packet of Tip Top biscuits and some Jojo chewing gum. We still had plenty of change, so Gino offered to buy me a beer at the *cabaret* tucked away in a recess of our street, beneath a parched flamboyant tree.

THE *CABARET* was the greatest institution in Burundi. The agora of the people. The radio of the pavement. The pulse of the nation. Every neighborhood, every street boasted these little huts without lights where, under cover of darkness, people came to drink a warm beer, perched uncomfortably on a bottle rack or a low stool barely off the ground. The *cabaret* offered drinkers the luxury of being there without being recognized, of choosing to join in conversations, or not, without being spotted. In this country, where everyone knew everyone, the *cabaret* was the only place you could speak your mind freely. It afforded the same freedom as a polling booth. And for a people who had never voted, lending your voice mattered. Whether you were a mighty *bwana* or a simple houseboy, hearts, heads, bellies, men and women were free to express themselves without pulling rank or status at the *cabaret*.

Gino ordered two bottles of Primus. He enjoyed going along to hear people talking politics. How many of us were sitting under the corrugated canopy of that little shack? Nobody knew and it didn't matter. The darkness plunged us into shadows from which only the occasional spoken word emerged here and there, at random, like a shooting star. Between each contribution, the pauses lasted an eternity. Then a fresh voice would rise up out of the void, skimming the surface before fading to silence again.

"I'm telling you, democracy is a force for good. At last the people will be able to determine their own fate. We should celebrate these presidential elections. They'll bring us peace and progress."

"My fellow compatriot, allow me to challenge your point of view. Democracy was invented by whites with the sole aim of dividing us. We've made a mistake in abandoning the single-party system. It took those whites centuries and many conflicts to reach the point where they are today. And now they're asking us to achieve the same thing in the space of a few months. I fear our leaders are sorcerers' apprentices, toying with a concept they only dimly understand."

"The man who doesn't know how to climb the tree remains on the ground."

"I'm still thirsty . . ."

"Culturally, it's ingrained in us to worship one king. One boss, one party, one nation! That unity is our motto."

"The dog cannot a cow become."

"This bloody thirst of mine is unquenchable . . ."

"It's a fake unity. We need to develop the cult of the people, which is the only guarantee of an enduring peace."

"Without preliminary work in the area of justice, my fear is that peace, which is the necessary framework for democracy, will simply be impossible! Thousands of our brothers were slaughtered in '72, but not a single trial took place. If nothing is done, the sons will end up avenging their fathers."

"Nonsense! Don't stir up the past, the future is a step

forward. Death to ethnic grouping, tribalism, regionalism, and antagonism!"

"And alcoholism!"

"I'm thirsty, I'm thirsty, I'm thirsty, I'm thirsty, I'm thirsty, I'm thirsty, I'm thirsty . . ."

"My brothers, God is with us every step of the way, just as he accompanied his son to Golgotha . . ."

"Aha, now I understand! It's that woman who's making me thirsty. I need another beer."

"Those whites will have triumphed with their Machiavellian scheme. They palmed off their God onto us, as well as their language and their democracy. Today, we seek out medical treatment in their countries and send our children to study in their schools. All Negroes are damned or deranged . . ."

"She's cleaned me out, that bitch, but she can't take away my thirst."

"We're living on the site of tragedy. Africa is shaped like a revolver. The facts are staring us in the face and there's nothing we can do. We've got to leave! Head north, or wherever, but we've got to leave!"

"The future comes from the past, like the egg from the chicken."

"Beer! beer! beer! beer! beer! beer! beer! beer! beer! beer! beer! beer! beer!"

We stayed a while longer, downing our warm Primuses in silence, and then I whispered goodbye in Gino's ear. With the alcohol coursing through my veins, I wasn't sure whether the shadow next to me was even his. But I had to get back. Papa would start worrying. I made my way home in the dark, staggering slightly. Hooting noises descended from the branches. There was a clear sky overhead, and through the darkness those nocturnal words still reached me. They can talk, the drunks at the *cabaret*, just as they like to listen, to prise the caps off beers and thoughts. Theirs are interchangeable spirits, floating voices, erratic heartbeats. In the ashen hours of night, individuals disappear and all that remains is the country talking to itself.

12

FRODEBU. UPRONA. THOSE WERE THE NAMES OF THE two major political parties contesting the presidential election on June 1, 1993, after thirty years of one-party rule by Uprona. They were the only two words we heard all day long: on the radio, on the television, from the mouths of grown-ups. Seeing as Papa didn't want us taking an interest in politics, I listened in elsewhere when people were talking about it.

Across the country, the electoral campaign felt like a big party. Uprona members wore red-and-white T-shirts and caps, and when they came across fellow supporters they made a sign by raising their three middle fingers. Frodebu followers chose green and white, and their rallying symbol was a raised fist. Everywhere, in public squares, in parks, and in stadiums, they sang and danced and laughed and organized noisy happenings. The only word on the lips of Prothé, our cook, was democracy. He had always been so serious, with that hangdog look of his, but even he had changed. Sometimes I would catch him in the kitchen wiggling his skinny backside and singing in a shrill voice: "Frodebu Komera! Frodebu Komera!" ("Frodebu okay!") It was inspiring to see the high spirits that politics produced. The upbeat energy felt like Sunday-morning football matches. I found it increasingly hard to fathom why Papa refused to let children talk about this joyousness, this wind of change that played havoc with people's hairstyles and filled their hearts with hope.

The day before the elections, I was sitting on the kitchen steps in the backyard of our house, squeezing the dog's ticks and removing its Cayor worms. Prothé was crouched down doing the laundry in front of the enamel sink, humming a religious song. After filling a big bowl with water and the contents of a box of OMO washing powder, he plunged the pile of dirty linen into the blue solution. Donatien sat on a chair opposite us, polishing his shoes. He wore a charcoal-gray *abacost* and a plastic comb in his hair.

Innocent was taking a shower a little farther off, at the end of the garden. His head and feet poked out from the piece of rusty corrugated iron we used as a door for the shower area. To annoy Prothé he'd made up a song that mocked the Frodebu party, and he was singing it at the top of his voice. "Fro-de-bu in-the-poo! U-pro-na: you-betch-ya!"

"He can be as childish as he likes," grumbled Prothé, glancing anxiously at Innocent to check whether he could be overheard, "but they won't win this time. I'm telling you, Donatien: they're blinded by thirty years of power, and their defeat will be even more bitter as a result."

"It's sinful to be presumptuous, my friend. Innocent is young and arrogant, and your wisdom should set an example. Don't be distracted by his puerile taunting."

"You're right, Donatien. But I still can't wait to see his face when he finds out we've won."

Innocent emerged bare-chested from his shower and slunk toward us like a cat. The droplets of water in his frizzy hair glistened in the sunlight, giving him a white skullcap. He stopped in front of Prothé, who looked down and scrubbed the laundry with renewed vigor. Innocent dug a hand in his pocket and fished out one of his stupid toothpicks, which he tossed into his mouth. He flexed his muscles and posed to impress us, while staring contemptuously at the back of Prothé's neck.

"Hey, you, houseboy!"

Prothé stopped scrubbing. He pulled himself up to his full height and held Innocent's eye with cold defiance. Donatien trailed off polishing his shoes. I let go of the dog's paw. Innocent couldn't believe that frail Prothé was standing up to him. Caught off-guard by the cook's self-assurance, Innocent eventually gave a small, faintly embarrassed smirk, spat his toothpick onto the ground and walked away, making the Uprona sign above his head, his three middle fingers raised. Prothé watched him saunter off. Once Innocent had disappeared behind the gates, Prothé went back to his enamel bowl and began humming to himself: "Frodebu Komera . . ."

13

IT WAS A TYPICAL MORNING. THE COCKEREL WAS CROW-
ing. The dog was scratching behind his ear. The aroma of coffee wafted through the house. The parrot mimicked Papa's
voice. We could hear the sound of a broom scraping the ground
in next door's yard, and the strains of a radio blaring somewhere in the neighborhood. A brightly colored agama lizard
was sunbathing, while a column of ants transported the grains
of sugar that Ana had spilt from the table. A morning just like
any other.

But this was also a day for making history. Across the country, people were getting ready to vote for the first time in their
lives. From first light, they had begun making their way to the
nearest polling stations. A never-ending procession of women
wearing colorful *pagnes*, and men carefully dressed in their
Sunday best, was moving along the main road, where minibuses full to bursting with euphoric voters paraded past. On
the football pitch near our house, people were flooding in from
every direction. Voting tables and polling booths had been
set up on the grass. Through the fencing, I watched the long
queue of voters, calm and law-abiding, waiting in the sunshine.
There were those in the crowd who couldn't contain their joy.
An old woman, dressed in a red wax-print cotton skirt and a
Jean-Paul II T-shirt, danced out of the polling booth singing:

"Democracy! Democracy!" A group of young people lifted her off the ground amid cheers. The presence of whites and Asians, wearing multi-pocket utility vests with "International Observers" written on the back, was noticeable in all four corners of the pitch. Burundians were conscious of the significance of this moment, of the beginning of a new era. This election would bring an end to the one-party system and military coups. Individuals were free at last to choose their representatives.

By the day's end, when the last voters had left, the pitch resembled a vast battlefield. The grass had been trampled underfoot. The ground was littered with discarded papers. Ana and I slipped under the fencing and crawled as far as the polling booths, where we gathered up the forgotten ballot papers for Frodebu, Uprona, and the People's Reconciliation Party (PRP). I wanted to keep a souvenir of such a momentous occasion.

THE FOLLOWING day felt strange. Nothing stirred. The city was anxiously awaiting the results. At home, the telephone didn't stop ringing. Papa wouldn't let me go out to see my friends. Our watchman had disappeared, the garden was empty, and there were very few cars on the road. It was all in such contrast to the elation of the day before.

During Papa's siesta, I escaped through the back door. I wanted to speak to Armand who was bound to have some information, courtesy of his father. I knocked at the gates and asked the houseboy to call for him. When Armand appeared, he told me his father was pacing the house, smoking cigarillos and putting a lot more sugar in his tea than usual. Their telephone, like ours, kept ringing. He told me to go straight back home and not to hang about in the street, because nobody knew what might happen. There were worrying rumors going around.

Shortly before nightfall, the three of us were sitting in the living room, Papa, Ana, and I, when someone rang my father and told him to switch on the radio. It was dark, Ana was biting her nails, and Papa was trying to tune into the right station. He found the frequency just as the Burundi National Radio and Television newscaster announced that the results were about to be declared. We heard the hissing of an old tape, followed by a brass band that accompanied a choir singing at the top of its voice: *"Burundi Bwacu, Burundi Buhire . . ."* After the national anthem, the Minister of the Interior began to speak. He declared victory for Frodebu. Papa didn't react. He just lit a cigarette.

There wasn't a single shout of joy in the neighborhood, no tooting of horns, no firecrackers. I thought I could hear distant clamoring up in the hills. Was it my imagination? With his obsession for keeping us out of politics, Papa holed himself up in his bedroom to make phone calls. Through the door, I caught snatches of phrases I didn't really understand. "This isn't a democratic victory, it's an ethnic reflex. . . . You know better than I do how things work in Africa, the Constitution has no weight. . . . The army supports Uprona. . . . In countries like this, you don't win an election without being the army's candidate. . . . I don't share your optimism. . . . They'll pay for this, sooner or later . . ."

We ate an early supper. I had made an onion omelet, and Ana served us slices of pineapple with Clarisse Sisters strawberry yogurts. Before going to bed, we watched the news in Papa's bedroom. The image was fuzzy: it was snowing on the channel. I wiggled the coathanger-aerial above the TV set.

Seated in front of the Burundian flag, the outgoing president, Major Pierre Buyoya, said in a measured voice: "I solemnly accept the verdict of the people and I invite the population to do likewise." I immediately thought of Innocent. Next, our new president, Melchior Ndadaye, appeared on the screen and announced calmly: "This is a victory for all Burundians." At which point I thought of Prothé. Finally, the chief of staff spoke: "The army respects democracy based on the multiparty system." And that's when I thought of Papa's words on the telephone.

I was in the middle of brushing my teeth when I heard Ana scream. I rushed into our bedroom to find her standing on my bed, clinging to the curtains. Below her, on the tiled floor, a scolopendra was crawling along the middle of the room. "Piece of filth!" Papa shouted, crushing the giant centipede.

As I clambered into bed, I asked Papa whether having a new president was good news.

"We'll see," came his reply.

Dear Laure,

The people have voted. On the radio, they said there was 97.3% turnout. That means everybody minus children, sick people in hospital, offenders in prison, madmen in asylums, bandits wanted by the police, lazybones who stayed in bed, people with no arms who can't hold a ballot paper and foreigners like my father, my mother and Donatien, who have the right to live and work here, but not to express their opinion, which has to remain where they come from. The new president is called Melchior, after one of the three wise kings. Some people love him, like Prothé, our cook. He says it's a victory for the people. Others hate him, like Innocent, our driver, but don't worry, that's just because he's moody and a bad loser.

I think the new president looks like he means business: he stands tall and doesn't put his elbows on the table or interrupt when people are talking. He wears a tie and a well-ironed shirt and he speaks politely. He's presentable and clean. This matters! Because soon he'll have his portrait hung throughout the country, so nobody forgets about him. It would be annoying to have a president who looked sloppy, or who had a squint, staring out of his photo-portrait in the ministries, airports, insurance companies, police stations, hotels, hospitals, cabarets, maternity wards, barracks, restaurants, hair salons, and orphanages.

Talking of which, I wonder where they've put the portraits of the ex-president? Have they thrown them away? Perhaps there's somewhere they can keep them, in case he decides to come back one day?

This is the first time we've had a president who isn't from the military. I don't think this job will be as much of a headache for him as it was for his predecessors. Military presidents always suffer from migraines. It's like they've got two brains. They never know whether to make peace or wage war.

Gaby

14

THE REPTILE WAS SPRAWLED OUT ON THE GRASS AT THE bottom of the garden. It had taken ten men, using ropes and bamboo poles, to lift the beast out of the van. News spread fast along our street and in no time a curious mob had gathered around the lifeless crocodile. A pair of yellow eyes, still open, with vertical black slashes for pupils, conspired eerily to make it look like it was watching us. The mortal blow to the top of its head was marked by a wound the size of a rosebud. Jacques, specially over from Zaire, had shot it with a single bullet. A week earlier, a Canadian tourist had been walking along the beach of her lakeside resort when a croc had carried her off. The local authorities had reacted as they always did, by dispatching a retaliatory operation. Papa and I went along for the adventure as privileged spectators. Jacques had led crocodile-hunting expeditions like this for years, with a small team of white men who were big-game enthusiasts. We boarded the motorboat at the sailing club, along with our ammunition and sniper rifles, and hugged the coast as far as the mouth of the Rusizi, where the muddy river joins the turquoise waters of Lake Tanganyika. As we headed slowly back up the delta, the hunters kept a finger on the trigger and a sharp eye on the scattered pods of hippopotamuses, fearing that a solitary male might charge at any moment. The noise of the engine was muffled by a cheeping colony of weaverbirds, whose nests dangled from the branches of the acacia trees. The men squinted in the sunlight and surveyed our surroundings using binoculars, their Winchester rifles to hand. Through the viewfinder of his gun, Jacques spotted the crocodile on a sandbank. It was sunbathing in the early-afternoon light, jaws wide open, while a crocodile bird dutifully cleaned its teeth. Jacques fired and a flock of whistling ducks rose up from the rushes by the riverbank. The shot rang out like the snap of dry wood. Felled at rest, the beast scarcely had time to move. Its jaw closed in slow motion. The little bird hopped around his friend for a few seconds, as if paying his final respects, before flying off into the distance to tend to another mouth.

ONCE THE bystanders had departed from our garden, we laid the beast on its back and Jacques methodically cut it up. He transferred the lumps of meat into plastic bags, which Prothé stored in the big freezer in the garage. Night was falling, but nothing was ready. The gardener helped Donatien put out the tables and chairs. Innocent carried the charcoal for the barbecue. Gino lit the Chinese lanterns hanging from the rubber fig tree and Papa unrolled an extension lead so we could set up the hi-fi in the garden. Ana was responsible for arranging the anti-mosquito coils under the tables. It was a special evening: we were celebrating my eleventh birthday!

When the music began wafting out of the speakers, all the locals were rounded up again. Attracted by the prospect of free booze, the drunks made an exception and deserted our local *cabaret*. The garden was quickly filled with the hubbub of voices combined with the boom of the subwoofers. I felt as if I was going to burst with happiness, caught in the throng of all those comings and goings, in our improvised bar beneath the moon, where the mood was festive and tears gave way to laughter.

It was the beginning of the summer holidays and things had got off to a positive start. I'd heard from Laure: *"Hi Gaby! I'm having a fab time by the sea with my cousins and my little brother. Thanks for your letter, what you wrote was really funny. Don't forget about me during the holidays. Bye for now. Love, Laure."*

On the back of the postcard was a selection of mini-photos from the Vendée: a chateau at Noirmoutier, high-rise hotels at Saint-Jean-de-Monts, a beach at Notre-Dame-de-Monts, a line of rocks at Saint-Hilaire-de-Riez. I read and reread that postcard dozens of times, always with the feeling that I was someone special for Laure. She had asked me not to forget her, and not a day went by without me thinking about her. In my next letter, I wanted to tell her how much she meant to me, that for the first time I felt I could share my feelings with someone, that I hoped to write to her for the rest of my life and that I even planned to visit her in France one day.

The other good news at the start of the holidays was that my parents were back on speaking terms, after months of cold war. They had congratulated me on successfully moving up to senior school. "We're proud of you," they had chorused: the "we" of a couple, of reunification. I lived in hope.

Pacifique had telephoned from Rwanda to wish me a happy birthday. He told me that peace talks were underway again, that he was well, that he missed us and wished he could be with us on my big day. After arriving in Rwanda, he had fallen head over heels in love with a girl and had just got engaged to her. He was impatient to introduce her to the family. She was called Jeanne, and Pacifique described her as the most beautiful woman in the entire African Great Lakes region. Then he confided something to me over the phone: once the war was over, he was going to launch his singing career, writing his own love songs and celebrating the beauty of his bride-to-be.

Life was sorting itself out, things were falling into place, and that evening I relished being surrounded by the people I loved and who loved me.

Out on the main terrace, Jacques was regaling a spellbound audience with the story of the crocodile hunt. He was really getting into his stride, puffing up his chest and rolling his "r"s with that Belgian accent of his. Like a movie actor unsheathing a revolver from its holster, he pulled out his silver Zippo from his pocket to light the cigarettes that dangled carelessly from the corner of his mouth. This worked its magic on Madame Economopoulos, who was enthralled by his charisma and wit. She kept showering him with compliments, which he was only too pleased to accept; while his jokes prompted peals of laughter from her, as she swooned like a teenage girl in love. Neither of them could believe they hadn't met before, and they embarked on some lengthy reminiscing about the good old days when Bujumbura was still called Usumbura, with its Grand Hotel, the dances and jazz orchestras at the Paguidas Hotel, the Kit Kat Cinema, and the sight of handsome American cars—Cadillacs and Chevrolets—in the city's streets. They spoke of their shared passion for orchids, for fine wines from faraway Europe, of the mysterious disappearance of the French television presenter Philippe de Dieuleveult and his camera crew close to the Inga Dam, of Mount Nyiragongo erupting and its majestic lava flows, of the gentle climate and stunning lakes and rivers . . .

Prothé moved among the guests, plying them with beer and grilled crocodile steak.

"Yuck!" said Innocent with a look of disgust, rejecting a plate offered to him by the cook. "Only whites and Zaireans eat crocodiles and frogs. You'd never see a real Burundian touch those bush animals! We're a civilized people!"

"It's very simple." Donatien beamed back at him, his mouth dripping with crocodile fat. "Burundians lack taste, and whites squander their money. Take the French, for example, they have no idea how to eat frogs, they make do with the legs!"

Over by the hi-fi, Armand was teaching Ana a few Soukous dance steps and she was rising to the challenge: she had wrapped a *pagne* round her bottom, which she wiggled without moving the rest of her body. The drunks were cheering her on. In the middle of the dance floor, under a spotlight besieged by insects, the twins' parents were dancing slowly, cheek to cheek, as if recalling their courting days, back in the time of the mythical Grand Kallé Orchestra. The twins' mother was much taller and stronger than their father. She led the dance while he kept his eyes closed and contorted his mouth like a dreaming puppy. The sweat made their shirts cling to their backs and traced circles under their armpits.

Papa exuded cheer and good humor. Unusually for him, he was wearing a tie and a hint of aftershave, and the way he'd combed his hair back brought out his irresistible green eyes. As for Maman, she shone in her flowery chiffon dress, sparking desire in men's gazes when she walked by. On more than one occasion, I even caught Papa staring at her. He was sitting on the edge of the dance floor, discussing business and politics with Armand's father, who had just returned from Saudi Arabia and was, by the look of things, making up for a long month without alcohol. Next to them, Armand's mother, dressed like the most pious woman in the parish, was nodding every now and again and raising her eyebrows at regular intervals. It was impossible to tell whether she was agreeing with her husband's views about Burundian coffee prices stabilizing on the London stock exchange, or saying her rosary for the umpteenth time that day.

I was stretched out on the hood of our pick-up, flanked by Gino and the twins, when we spotted Francis gate-crashing the party. We couldn't believe our eyes! No sooner had he set foot on our land than Maman gave him a bottle of Fanta and offered him one of the plastic chairs under the rubber fig tree.

"Gaby, can you see what I see?" thundered Gino. "You've got to tell that shithead where to go! He has no business at your birthday party."

"Nothing I can do about it, bro. My dad said the party was open to everyone from around here."

"But not Francis! He's our worst enemy!"

"Maybe it's time to make peace with him," said the twins.

"You bunch of total losers," Gino fired back. "We don't do deals with scum like that, okay? We'll smash his ugly face in— that's what he deserves!"

"He's not hurting anyone right now," I said. "Let him drink his Fanta and we'll keep watch."

Nobody took their eyes off Francis, even for a second. He pretended not to see us, even though he was surveying everything as he checked out what was going down at the party. He scanned the guests menacingly, jiggling his left leg nervously. When he stood up to fetch another drink, he had a brief chat with Maman, who kept turning and pointing in my direction as if explaining that she was my mother. Then he flitted from group to group, striking up conversations here and there, including with Gino's dad.

"I don't believe it, he's talking to my old man! What the hell have they got to say to each other? I bet he's trying to get the lowdown on us, Gaby. He wants to pass himself off as one of us!"

We watched his little game at a distance. Innocent invited him to share a beer, and minutes later they were slapping each other on the back like old pals.

It was past midnight now, and the alcohol and darkness were having a combined effect. A group of shirtless French guys, in Buja on Voluntary National Service Overseas, played leapfrog in front of the drunks from the *cabaret*, who were entertained by the performance. A young man groped inside his girlfriend's bra as she chatted with her friend about the moral-education classes she taught at Stella Matutina primary school. An elderly Burundian man with a white beard, nick-named Gorbachev on account of the birthmark on his fore-head, stood on one leg reciting the courtly poetry of Pierre de Ronsard in front of the parrot's cage. A group of children was playing with the tame monkey that belonged to an effeminate Flemish man who lived on our street. He went by the name of Fifi and always wore African wax-print shirts as well as *bou-bous*, flowing wide-sleeved robes. There were stacks of empty crates piled up on the kitchen steps. Prothé and Donatien kept making trips to return the bottles to the kiosk.

Time for us to find a quiet corner, safe from parental eyes, in the unlit area of the garden. We sat down on the grass, under the Chinese lanterns hanging from the rubber fig, to share a few cigarettes and watch the dance floor unobserved.

"Shit, I just trod on something!" said Armand, who had brought along the two bottles of Primus he'd hidden in the pot of tree ferns when no one was looking.

"Yeah, watch out, that'll be the crocodile carcass," I ex-plained.

During a lull in the music we heard the unmistakable sounds of chewing and swallowing: Madame Economopoulos's dachshunds were tucking into the remains of the reptile. They enjoyed their feast in the dark, while my friends raised a toast to my eleventh birthday.

"The dachshunds are gonna be flaunting it when they tell the other mutts they've eaten croc!" said Gino.

We all burst out laughing, except for Armand, who had noticed someone heading toward us.

"Who's there?" I asked, stubbing out my cigarette and waving the smoke away.

"It's me, Francis."

"There's nothing for you here," answered Gino, leaping to his feet. "Get lost!"

"It's a neighborhood party, and I live in the 'hood! Gotta problem with that?"

"Look, this is my friend's birthday, and you're not invited. Like I said, get lost!"

"Who's talking? I can't see. Is it Kojak's son? The Belgian with the comb-over! What's your name again?"

"Gino! And watch what you say when you're talking about my parents."

"Your parents? I only mentioned your dad. Where's your mum, by the way? I've seen everyone's parents except for her . . ."

"Come to spy on us?" said Armand. "Doing a spot of detective work, hey, Columbo?"

"You're not wanted here," insisted Gino. "Clear off!"

"No! I'm staying!"

Gino head-butted Francis in the stomach. They stumbled over the disembowelled crocodile in the dark. The dogs started barking. I ran to warn the grown-ups while Armand hid our cigarettes and beers. Jacques and Papa arrived with a torch. When they finally managed to separate Francis and Gino, all smeared with crocodile innards, Francis was accused of deliberately starting a fight. Papa caught him by the collar and threw him off our land, at which point a humiliated Francis lobbed stones at our gate and shouted that we'd all pay for this. Our little gang gave him the finger and then, to loud whooping from the group of French volunteers, we turned round and dropped our trousers. Everybody was falling about laughing, until Jacques shouted: "Shit, where's my Zippo? Where's my Zippo?"

All thoughts turned to Francis.

"Catch that bastard!" shouted Gino.

Papa sent Innocent after the interloper, but he came back empty-handed.

Then all at once the incident was over and the party became more raucous than ever. It was in full swing when a power cut struck. A hundred dancing guests came to an abrupt halt, letting out a frustrated "Argh!" Drenched in sweat, they clamored for music by stamping their feet, clapping their hands and shouting my name: "Gaby! Gaby!" Everyone was up for a big night, and a power cut wasn't going to stop them. Someone suggested carrying on with live music. So Donatien and Innocent rushed off to fetch some neighborhood drums, the twins brought their father's guitar, and one of the French guys produced a trumpet from the trunk of his Renault 4. There was a pleasant breeze now and a light rain starting to fall. In the distance, on the shores of the lake, we could hear the dull rumble of thunder rolling closer. This worried some people, especially the older folks, who recommended bringing the tables and chairs inside, ahead of the downpour. Donatien cut short the discussion by improvising some *brakka* music on the guitar. Tentatively, people began to move their bodies once more, against the black sky streaked with flashes of lightning. The crickets fell quiet as the drunks clinked their bottles with forks and teaspoons to accompany the melody. When the trumpet joined the guitar, it was welcomed by catcalls and whoops of joy. The guests were dancing with even more passion now. The dogs were terrified, tails between legs, flattening themselves under the tables just seconds before the sky exploded—sound-effects, lightning, gusts of wind, the patter of rain. The drummers came onstage, picking up the pace. Nobody could resist the furious tempo of the music, which possessed our bodies like a friendly spirit. The trumpet was doing its breathless best to follow the rhythm set by the percussion. Prothé and Innocent were hitting the stretched drum skins in unison, their faces strained, a thick sweat sliding down their gleaming foreheads. The guests' hands marked the beat as their feet hammered out the counter-rhythm, kicking up the heavy dust in the yard. The music was as quick as our throbbing temples. The banging and beating swelled as one. The wind swayed the garden treetops, making leaves quiver and branches rustle. There was electricity in the atmosphere, as the smell of damp earth filled the air. A warm downpour was about to come crashing down on us, so violently that we would run to collect the tables, chairs and plates before sheltering under the safety of our *barza* to watch the party dissolving in a cloudburst. Soon my birthday would be over, but I chose to savor that minute before the rain came down in earnest, that taste of suspended happiness as music joined our hearts and filled the space between us, celebrating life, this moment in time, the eternity of my eleven years, here, beneath the cathedral that was the rubber fig tree of my child-hood, and deep down I knew that everything would turn out all right.

15

SUMMER HOLIDAYS ARE WORSE THAN BEING UNEMployed. We stayed put for two months, kicking our heels and trying to fill our dreary days. Even if we messed around and had a laugh from time to time, there was no getting away from it: we were as bored as Komodo dragons. It was dry season, so the river was down to a trickle and it was impossible to cool off. The mangoes, which had shriveled in the heat, were unsellable, and it was too far for us to head over to the sailing club every afternoon.

It was a relief when school started again. Papa dropped me off in front of the senior entrance. Now that I was eleven, I attended the *collège*, where I was in the same class as all my friends: a new life was opening up. Some days we had lessons in the afternoon as well, and I was discovering new subjects like science, English, chemistry, and art. Those students who spent their holidays in Europe or America had come back with the latest clothes and shoes. At first, I didn't pay any attention. Gino and Armand couldn't stop talking about it, though, with shining eyes. Their envy was becoming an obsession, and eventually it infected me, too. It wasn't about marbles and marble-runs anymore, but clothes and brands. The trouble was, in order to keep up you needed money. Lots of money. Even if we'd sold all the mangoes in the neighborhood, we still couldn't have afforded those trainers with the mini-swoosh on them.

The students who had returned from *over there*—from Europe and America—described shops that were several kilometers long and overflowing with trainers, T-shirts, sports shirts, and jeans. There was nothing in Buja, apart from the empty Bata shop window in the town center, and the stalls at Jabe market offering Reebok Pumps with holes in them and designer brands with spelling mistakes. We felt deprived of all the things we'd done without up until then. And this feeling changed something inside us. We harbored a silent hatred toward those who did own such things.

Donatien, who had noticed my new attraction to brands, as well as my readiness to bad-mouth certain rich kids at school, informed me that envy was a deadly sin. But his attempts at moral education went over my head and for once I preferred talking to Innocent, who had ways of getting hold of the accessories I was dreaming of, and on the cheap, too. At school, groups were formed according to new criteria: those with desirable possessions kept to themselves.

Armand was the exception to the rule. He didn't have any designer clothes or aftershaves, but he made everyone laugh. This meant he could cross the invisible barriers separating one student from another, and be accepted by the in-crowd. Gino grew bitter when he saw Armand in the playground, close to the refreshment stall, chatting with his new friends.

We talked about it one evening as we lay on the night watchman's mat, under the frangipani tree, dipping slices of green mango into coarse salt.

"Armand is a traitor. He barely talks to us at school, but as soon as he's back home we're best friends again."

"He's making the most of it—you'd do exactly the same.

He's been invited to all the parties since the beginning of term. The twins even told me he kissed a girl on the mouth!"

"For real?! With his tongue?"

"Dunno, but at least he's having a laugh, while we're stuck here. If I could do the same, I'd be there like a shot."

"What, so you're ashamed of our band of brothers, too?"

"No, it's not like that, Gino. You're all my best friends for life! But nobody takes any notice of us at school, and the girls won't even look at us, so—"

"One day they'll see us for who we are, Gaby, and then everybody'll be afraid of us."

"Why d'you want them to be afraid of us?"

"To be respected. Get it? That's what my mother's always saying. What matters is being respected."

I was astonished to hear Gino mention his mother. He never spoke about her. He kept a pile of envelopes with red, white, and blue edges on his bedside table, and sent them to her every week. But he never went to Rwanda, even though it was only a few hours' drive away, and she didn't come to Bujumbura, either. He said the political situation made things impossible for the time being, but that one day, when peace returned, he would go and live in a big house in Kigali with both his father and mother. It made me sad to think that Gino was ready to leave me, the band of brothers, and everyone on our street. Like Maman, Mamie, Pacifique, and Rosalie, Gino dreamed of the big Rwandan homecoming, and I pretended to share in that dream so as not to disappoint them. But secretly, I prayed for nothing to change, for Maman to come back home to us, for life to return to the way it used to be and stay like that forever.

As I was reflecting on all this, I heard a rumbling noise. Gino's father came running out of the house like a frightened sheep, shouting at us to stay away from the walls and follow him to the middle of the garden. We stood up thinking it was a joke—he looked like he'd just seen a ghost—and trotted after him, without realizing what had just happened. It was only when, a few minutes later, we saw the wide crack zigzagging down the length of the garage wall that we understood. The earth had moved imperceptibly beneath our feet. It did so every day in this country, in this corner of the world. We were living on the axis of the Great Rift, at the precise spot where Africa fractures.

The people of this region mirrored the land. Beneath the calm appearance, behind the facade of smiles and optimistic speeches, dark underground forces were continuously at work, fomenting violence and destruction that returned for successive periods, like bad winds: 1965, 1972, 1988. A glowering, uninvited ghost showing up at regular intervals to remind us that peace is merely a brief interlude between two wars. This poisonous lava, the thick flow of blood, was ready to rise to the surface once more. We didn't know it yet, but the hour of the inferno had come, and the night was about to unleash its cackle of hyenas and wild dogs.

16

I WAS SLEEPING LIGHTLY WHEN I FELT SOMETHING touching my head. At first, I thought that rats were chewing my curly hair, the way they used to before Papa laid traps all over the house. Then I heard a whisper: "Gaby, are you asleep?" Ana's voice woke me. I opened my eyes to find our bedroom plunged in darkness. I tugged the curtain with my left hand and a beam of moonlight shone through the mosquito net at the window, lighting up my little sister's petrified face.

"What can we hear, Gaby?"

I didn't understand. It was a peaceful night. There was just an owl hooting in the false ceiling above our bedroom. I sat up and waited, until I heard several dull cracking noises ring out in increasingly rapid succession.

"It sounds like gunfire . . ."

Ana slid into my bed and huddled against me. An agonizing silence followed the noise of explosions and machine-gun fire. Ana and I were alone in the house. Papa often spent the night away from home, and had done so for a while now: Innocent claimed that our father was seeing a young woman who lived in the street behind his house, in the modest district of Bwiza. It made me sad because, since they'd started talking again, I still had hopes of Maman and Papa getting back together.

I pressed the button that lit up my watch: the dial said two o'clock in the morning. With each explosion, Ana clung to me even more tightly.

"What's happening, Gaby?"

"I don't know . . ."

The shots petered out toward six in the morning. Papa still wasn't back. We got ourselves up and dressed before making sure our schoolbags were ready. Prothé wasn't at home, either. We laid the breakfast table out on the terrace. I made the tea. The parrot was doing somersaults in his cage. I went to see if there was anyone about on our land. Not a soul. Even the *zamu* had disappeared. We ate and cleared the table. I helped Ana do her hair. Still nobody. I kept an eye on the gates, since Papa's workers were due. Nothing stirred. We sat on the front steps waiting for Innocent and Papa to turn up. Ana took out her maths book from her schoolbag and started reciting her times tables. Not a single pedestrian or car on the road in front of the house. What was going on? Where was everybody? We could hear snatches of classical music nearby. It was Thursday, but the neighborhood was more dead than on a Sunday morning.

Finally, a car pulled up. I recognized the Pajero's horn and rushed over to open the gates. Papa wore a serious expression and there were bags under his eyes. He got out of the car and asked if we were all right. I nodded, but Ana was sulking, she wanted to give him a hard time for abandoning us all night. Papa headed straight to the living room and switched on the radio. We heard the same piece of music that had been wafting in and out of earshot before.

"Shit! Shit! Shit!" Papa kept saying over and over again, his head in his hands.

Later on, I discovered that it was traditional to play classical music during a military coup. On November 28, 1966, for Michel Micombero's coup, it was Schubert's piano sonata No.

95

21; on November 9, 1976, for Jean-Baptiste Bagaza's coup, it was Beethoven's 7th symphony; and on September 3, 1987, for Pierre Buyoya's coup, it was Chopin's Bolero in C major.

On this day, October 21, 1993, we were treated to Wagner's *Twilight of the Gods*. Papa secured the gates using a heavy chain and several padlocks. He ordered us not to leave the house and to stay away from the windows. Then he set up our mattresses in the hallway because of the risk of stray bullets. We spent the whole day lying on the floor. It was weird: like camping in our own house.

Papa shut himself in his bedroom, as usual, to make phone calls. At around three o'clock I was playing cards with Ana, and Papa was on the telephone, when I heard a scuffling noise coming from the kitchen. I tiptoed over to take a look. There, out of breath and standing behind the bars, was Gino.

"I can't open up," I whispered, "my father's double-locked the house. How did you get in here?"

"I slipped under the fencing. Anyway, I'm not staying. D'you know what's going on?"

"Yes, there's been a coup, we heard the classical music."

"The army has killed the new president."

"What? I don't believe you. . . . Swear you mean it!"

"I swear! A Canadian journalist called my father to tell him. It's a military coup. They also killed the president of the national assembly and other big *bwanas* from the government. . . . There are rumors that massacres have begun throughout the interior. Oh, and d'you want to know the best news of all?"

"What is it?"

"Attila's escaped!"

"Attila, the Von Gotzens' horse?"

"Yeah! Crazy, eh? Last night, a mortar bomb landed close

to the stables of the equestrian club, behind the president's official residence. A building caught fire. The horses panicked, Attila went nuts, he was rearing up and whinnying like he was deranged and then he started kicking down the door of his box: he smashed the lock and jumped the gates, before disappearing into the city. You should have seen Madame Von Gotzen this morning. She came round to ours in her nightie, with curlers in her hair and her eyes all puffy from crying. It was the funniest sight! She wanted my father to use his contacts to find her horse. 'There's been a military coup, Madame Von Gotzen,' he kept repeating, 'there's nothing I can do to help you—not even the president of the Republic was able to help himself.' But she wouldn't let it drop: 'Attila must be found! Contact the United Nations! The White House! The Kremlin!' She didn't care about the president being killed; that wrinkly old racist just wanted to talk about her stupid horse. They're too much, those colonial settlers! Their pets' lives matter more to them than human ones. Anyway, I'd better get going, Gaby. More news in the next update."

Gino ran off. He looked electrified, almost as if he were enjoying this turn of events. But I felt lost and unable to take in what was happening. Our president had just been assassinated. . . . I thought back to what Papa had said, on the day of Ndadaye's victory: "They'll pay for this, sooner or later."

That evening, we went to bed early. Papa was smoking more than usual. He had also brought his mattress into the hallway and he listened to the little radio set, stroking Ana's hair while she slept soundly. We had a single candle for light, and it blurred the shapes in the room.

Toward nine o'clock, the classical music stopped. A presenter began to speak, in French. He kept clearing his throat between sentences, his monotonous voice at odds with the gravity of the situation; you'd have thought he was announcing the results of a local volleyball competition.

"The National Council of Public Safety has taken the following decisions: there will be a curfew throughout the territory from eighteen hundred hours until six o'clock in the morning; all borders will be closed; the movement of persons from one municipality to another is forbidden; gatherings of more than three people are forbidden; the Council calls on the people to remain calm . . ."

I nodded off before the end of the list. I dreamed I was sleeping peacefully, suspended in a soft cloud of sulphur fumes produced by an erupting volcano.

17

WE SPENT SEVERAL DAYS SLEEPING IN THE HALLWAY, not even leaving the house by day. A gendarme from the French embassy called Papa to advise against venturing outside at all. Maman, who was living over at a friend's place in the hills above the city, telephoned us daily to catch up on the news. The radio reported widespread massacres in the center of the country.

School reopened the following week. The city was strangely calm. A few shops had raised their shutters, but the civil servants hadn't returned to work and ministers were still taking refuge in foreign embassies and in bordering countries. When we drove past the presidential palace, I could see the damage to the security wall. These were the only traces of fighting that were visible in town. In the playground, the students told stories about the night of the coup, about gunfire and the sound of mortar bombs, the death of the president and mattresses in hallways. Nobody was genuinely frightened, though. For privileged children like us, who lived in the city center and in residential neighborhoods, war was just a word. We heard things, but hadn't seen anything. Our life carried on much as it had before, with gossip about parties, crushes, clothes. The domestic staff in our houses, the employees of our parents, those who lived in poor neighborhoods, or in Bujumbura Rural Province, or in the interior, those who didn't receive security warnings from any embassy, and who didn't have a watchman to guard their house, or a driver to take their children to school, those who traveled on foot, by bike or local bus, they had the measure of what was really happening.

When I came back from school at lunchtime, Prothé was shelling peas on the kitchen table. I knew that he had voted for Ndadaye, and how sweet that victory had tasted to him. I hardly dared look at him.

"Hello, Prothé. How are you?"

"Forgive me, Monsieur Gabriel, but I don't have the strength to talk. They've murdered hope. They've murdered hope, that's all I can say. Truly, they have murdered hope . . ."

When I left the kitchen, he was still repeating those words.

After lunch, Donatien and Innocent drove me back to school. When we were level with the Muha bridge, we passed an army tank.

"Look at those soldiers," Donatien pointed out wearily, "they're lost. First they stage a coup, then they kill the president and now that the people are rising up and the interior of the country is being torn apart, they're backtracking and demanding the government return and put out the fire lit by the soldiers in the first place. Poor Africa . . . may God come to our rescue!"

Innocent didn't comment, he just concentrated on driving, staring straight ahead.

The days passed more quickly now, since the curfew forced everybody to be home by six o'clock, before nightfall. In the evenings, we slurped our soup while listening to the radio and its alarming news. I began to wonder about the meanings behind silences, about what some people left unsaid as well as the insinuations and predictions of others. The country was built on whispers and riddles. There were invisible rifts, sighs, and glances that I didn't understand.

As the days went by, war continued to rage in the countryside. Villages were ravaged and set alight, schools suffered grenade attacks and the students inside were burned alive. Hundreds of thousands of people were fleeing toward Rwanda, Zaire, and Tanzania. In Bujumbura, the talk was of clashes in the outlying districts. At night, we could hear the gunfire in the distance. Prothé and Donatien often failed to turn up for work because the army kept rounding up people in their neighborhood.

From the womb-like safety of our house, all of this seemed unreal. The *impasse* was as sleepy as ever. At siesta-time you could hear the birds chirruping in the branches, a breeze stirred the leaves and the venerable rubber fig trees offered welcome shade. Nothing had changed. We carried on playing and exploring. The heavy rains were back. The vegetation was lush and verdant once more. The trees bowed under the weight of ripe fruit, and the river flowed full.

One afternoon, when all five of us were out on a mango-hunting expedition, barefoot with rods in hand, Gino suggested venturing farther afield since we'd already raided our street. We found ourselves standing outside the fencing to Francis's house, and I had an uneasy feeling.

"Let's not stay here, it'll just end in trouble."

"Don't be a scaredy-cat, Gaby!" said Gino. "This mango tree has our name on it."

Armand and the twins stared at each other; they were in two minds, but Gino wouldn't let the idea go. So we made our way slowly up the gravel path, muffling our footsteps. There were no gates, making it easy to get onto Francis's plot. The house, which had been built on top of a hillock, looked sinister with its peeling walls and damp patches where the plaster on the veranda's dropped ceiling had blistered. We approached the mango tree, its branches spread over the entire garden. Dirty mosquito nets, behind the window bars, prevented us from glimpsing the inside of the house. The doors were closed and the place felt unnaturally quiet. We stopped at the foot of the tree and Gino knocked off one mango, then two, then three. His rod ruffled the leaves, which jostled like a party of hornbills, while I kept a lookout.

Suddenly, I thought I saw a shadow moving furtively behind the dusty mosquito nets. "Wait!" We froze, staring at the house. Silence. All we could hear was the river babbling at the bottom of the garden. Gino resumed picking off the mangoes. Armand cheered him on and danced the Soukous every time a fruit landed on the grass. The twins and I stayed on the alert. Behind us, a bird took flight with a rustling of wings. We spun round. Armand and the twins were the first to bolt, at the speed of light, in the direction of the road. Next, Gino made a run for it and I followed without a thought. We raced round the house and down the slope leading to the Muha. I was terrified of being caught. Still, I wasn't convinced that Francis was chasing us, so I glanced backward. That's when his fist smashed into my face and I hit the ground. The blows came fast and furious, like a swarm of wasps. Gino was shouting and trying to protect me. Then I saw him go down, too, centimeters from where I had landed. A hand dragged us over to the river's edge and Francis plunged our heads into the brown, silty waters. I couldn't breathe. My face was pressed against the riverbed. No matter how hard I struggled to break free, Francis's hand was like a vise crushing my neck. When he brought me back up to the surface, I caught snatches of what he was saying. "You shouldn't steal from other people's gardens. Didn't your parents ever teach you that?" Then he dunked me again, head first, with a fury that chilled my bones. Everything went blurry. My hands were flailing, trying in vain to grab hold of something, a branch, a buoy, a shred of hope . . . I clawed at the riverbed as if to find another way out, a hidden trapdoor. The water was seeping into my ears, into my nostrils, as the voice droned on in the background. It was so faint by contrast with the grip that held me underwater. "Bunch of spoiled brats, I'll teach you manners." As well as smothering me, Francis was trying to knock me out. My forehead kept hitting the bottom. My instinct was to find air as fast as possible. But where? My lungs were suffocating, shriveling up. My racing heart panicked, trying to escape through my mouth. I could hear the distant echo of my stifled cries. I was calling out for Papa and Maman. Where were they? Francis wasn't messing around. He had made up his mind to kill me, for real. So was this what violence meant? Raw fear and disbelief. "Your mothers are white men's bitches!" I heard, as he yanked my head out of the river. And then I was back under again. I was losing the battle. Slowly, my exhausted muscles began to relax as I resigned myself to these ten centimeters of water, I was slipping imperceptibly away, with Francis's voice to lull me. Fear and submission were mine; violence and strength his.

But Gino refused to drown. He put all his might into resisting the water and Francis's words. He could see further ahead. He still wanted to harvest mangoes in November and build rafts out of banana leaves for us to row downriver. He was neither paralyzed nor fascinated by this new kind of violence. He faced it down. He was at Francis's mercy and yet he behaved as if they were equals. He fired back, retaliated, counterattacked. I noticed the veins in his neck bulging like an inner tube. "Don't insult my mother! Don't insult my mother!"

I felt the pressure on my neck relax as Francis tried to contain Gino's mounting energy. He was using both arms, both hands, both knees pressed into my best friend's back. At last there was some air in my lungs again. I was on all fours at first, before collapsing onto my back, spluttering. The blue sky was so very bright. Dazzled by the sun, I closed my eyes and crawled over to prop my head against the trunk of a felled banana tree on the ground. One of my ears was blocked.

"Nobody has the right to insult my mother!" Gino kept saying.

"Oh yes, they do, I can say what I like. Your mother's a whore!"

Francis thrust Gino's head back into the brown water where I had wanted to surrender. It was siesta-time and the heat of the day had reached its peak. The road was deserted. There wasn't a single car over on the bridge. As I buried my dazed head in the spongy bark of the banana tree, I spat out yet more water and coughed up panicked words. Francis kept on talking, never drawing breath, like those washerwomen who plunge their laundry into the water while chatting about the weather. At the end of each of Francis's sentences, Gino's head disappeared into the foam of the river. "So where is she, your bitch of a mother? We never see her around . . ." Gino gulped a few mouthfuls of air before slipping back down, like the float of a fishing hook. He was yelling underwater, and this made the river eddy and swirl around his head. "Where is she, your bitch of a mother?" The more Francis repeated it, the more Gino risked suffocating, the more I shouted at Francis to let him go, and the more Francis kept asking the same question. Gino was losing his strength. He was giving up.

By the time I had finally come to my senses and got to my feet, to try and stop Francis, Gino stammered: "Dead." I heard the word, clearly. "My mother's dead," he said a second time, with a sob.

Over on the bridge, an old man in a black hat was leaning against the railings, a rainbow-colored umbrella unfurled above his head, its metal tip gleaming like a Christmas star. Old people enjoy watching children messing about in rivers. They know their days of playing like that are over. Francis waved at him. The old man didn't respond. He watched us a while longer before shuffling on his way, with his black hat and his colorful umbrella. Francis walked straight past me and I shrank back. He didn't even look at me, he just left. I went over to Gino, who was sobbing by the river's edge, his head between his legs as he cried into his sodden clothes. Everything seemed calm again. The water flowed by with cruel indifference. I put my hand on my friend's shoulder to comfort him. But Gino rebuffed me, standing up abruptly and heading in the direction of the road.

I sat by the water until my ear finally popped. Gradually, the sounds of traffic started up again. The bells on the Chinese bicycles, sandals scraping the beaten-earth pavement, the squish of minibus tires on warm asphalt. The city was returning to life. There was movement on the bridge. I felt an icy anger rising up inside me. The inside of my mouth was bleeding, and I had grazes on my hands and knees. I washed my wounds in the Muha.

My anger was telling me to defy my fear in order to stop it from growing. It was the same fear that made me give up too often. I decided to confront Francis. I went back to his garden to rescue our rods. There he was on the doorstep, threatening me as I walked over. But I carried on, the salty taste of blood on my tongue. Then I stopped and looked him in the eye for a long time. Behind that arrogant smile of his, he didn't flinch. He just stayed there on the threshold of his house. I had been scared of him when my head was in the water. Not anymore, though. I could taste the blood in my mouth, but it was nothing—nothing compared to Gino's tears. All I had to do was swallow the blood and its taste would be forgotten. But Gino's tears? Anger had rushed in to replace my fear. I was no longer afraid of what might happen to me. I picked up our rods and left the mangoes behind. Nobody would collect them now. I knew that, and it didn't matter. There was a rising tide of anger inside me and I couldn't have cared less about those mangoes rotting in the fresh grass.

18

GINO AVOIDED ME AFTER THAT. ARMAND AND THE
twins had no idea what had happened down by the river. I
let them think we'd got away safely, like they did. But I was
haunted by Gino's tears. Was his mother really dead? I couldn't
bring myself to ask him outright. Not yet. We were living
through uncertain times. The weeks were like the sky during
rainy season: each day brought with it fresh rumors, violence,
and safety directives. The country still had no president and
part of the government was living in hiding. But in the *cabarets*,
people drank their beers and ate their goat-meat skewers as if
making a stand against tomorrow's worries.

The capital had been seized by a new phenomenon. We
called these days "lockdowns." Flyers were distributed across
the city with messages advising people not to leave home on one
or more specific days. When these operations were underway,
gangs of youths headed for the streets with the blessing of the
police. They erected blockades on the main roads in different
neighborhoods, attacking and throwing stones at any cars or
passersby that dared to venture out. Fear came crashing down
on the city. Shops were shut, schools remained closed, street
hawkers disappeared, and everyone barricaded themselves inside their homes. The morning after these days of paralysis,

corpses were counted in the ditches, stones were cleared from the roads, and life resumed its usual rhythm.

Papa felt powerless. Having tried so hard to distance us from politics, he was now incapable of protecting us from what was going on in the country. He looked haggard, and he worried about his children and his business. He had halted work at his construction sites, due to the large-scale massacres taking place in the country's interior—there was talk of fifty thousand deaths—and he'd had to lay off most of his workers.

One morning, while I was at school, a violent argument broke out on our land between Prothé and Innocent, in full view of Papa. I never discovered what it was about, but Innocent raised his hand against Prothé. Papa fired Innocent on the spot for refusing to apologize, and for continuing to threaten everybody.

The permanent tension made people nervous. They became sensitive to the slightest noise, kept their guard up in the street, looked in the rear-view mirror to check they weren't being followed. Everyone was in a state of high alert. One day, in the middle of a geography lesson, a tire blew out on boulevard de l'Indépendance, just outside the school walls, and our entire class, including the teacher, dived under our desks.

At school, relationships between the Burundian students had changed, subtly, but in ways I grew conscious of. There were lots of cryptic comments, as well as secret codes. When we needed to get into groups, for sport or to prepare a presentation in class, our sense of unease was quick to surface. I couldn't explain this cruel shift, this tangible sense of confusion.

That is, until break-time one day, when two Burundian boys started fighting behind the main playground, hidden from the view of teachers and supervisors. The other Burundian students, wading into the hot waters of the dispute, promptly divided into two groups, each supporting one of the boys. "Filthy Hutus!" shouted one side. "Filthy Tutsis!" replied the other.

That afternoon, for the first time in my life, I entered the dark reality of this country. I was a direct witness to Hutu–Tutsi antagonism, the line that could not be crossed, forcing everyone to belong to one camp or the other. This camp was something you were born with, like a child's given name, something that followed you forever. Hutu or Tutsi. It had to be one or the other. Heads or tails. From that day on, I was like a blind person who had regained their sight, as I began to decipher people's body language and glances, words left unspoken and ways of behaving that had previously passed me by.

War always takes it upon itself, unsolicited, to find us an enemy. I wanted to remain neutral, but I couldn't. I was born with this story. It ran in my blood. I belonged to it.

19

WE DISCOVERED AN EVEN MORE VIOLENT REALITY IN
Rwanda, which we visited at the end of the February holidays,
when we attended Pacifique's wedding. My uncle had announced the news only a week earlier, after growing insecurity
in Kigali had accelerated matters. Maman, Ana, and I were
representing the family: Mamie and Rosalie had to stay behind
in Bujumbura, since their refugee status meant they couldn't
travel.

In the arrivals hall of Grégoire-Kayibanda airport we were
met by Eusébie, Maman's aunt, who was barely older than
Maman and who had always refused to go into exile. Maman
thought of her as the big sister she'd never had. Aunt Eusébie
was as pale-skinned as I was. Her long face resembled those
of the women in our family, she had a wide domed forehead,
tiny ears, a slender neck, a gap between her slightly protruding
front teeth, and a sprinkling of freckles on her nose and eyelids.
She wore a black pleated skirt down to her ankles and a jacket
with big shoulder pads that made her look like a scarecrow.
Ana had spent a week as a guest in her home when she had
visited with Maman, but I was meeting her for the first time.
She was overcome and hugged me tightly against her soft skin,
which smelled of shea butter.

Aunt Eusébie was a widow who lived in a house in the

center of Kigali where, single-handedly, she raised her four children—three girls and a boy, aged five to sixteen—Christelle, Christiane, Christian, and Christine.

Aunt Eusébie's daughters rushed to greet Ana and wouldn't let go of her. She was their guest of honor, the doll they wanted to pamper in the coming days. They argued over who got to spend the most time with her and fought to brush her smooth hair, which seemed so exotic to them. On the walls of their bedroom, they had stuck up the photos they'd taken a year earlier with Ana, during the Christmas holidays.

Christian, who was my age, stared playfully at me with his twinkling eyes. He was almost as talkative as the twins, and his curiosity was in a league of its own. He asked a thousand and one questions about Burundi, my friends, and my favorite sports. As the proud captain of his school football team, he insisted on showing me the cups and medals he had won at the inter-schools' championships and which were displayed on the big chest of drawers in the living room. He couldn't wait for the next Africa Cup of Nations, which was being held in Tunisia. His favorite team, Cameroon, hadn't qualified, so he had decided to support Nigeria.

Over dinner, Aunt Eusébie told us all sorts of funny stories that made Maman giggle uncontrollably. My aunt was hilarious when it came to recounting the holidays she and Maman had spent as teenagers with the Girl Scouts in the Burundian countryside. She transformed the trials and tribulations of our family into comic tales and fantastic adventures, egged on affectionately by her children. They applauded and encouraged, sometimes finishing off the stories for her or helping her to find the right word in French. After dinner, Aunt Eusébie told us to get ready for bed and our cousins jumped up happily and noisily. The girls used their toothbrushes as microphones in the bathroom, singing and dancing in front of the large mirror. Christian had put on his Roger Milla shirt instead of pajamas. Before going to sleep, he liked to kick a ball against his bedroom wall, which was covered in footballer posters. He claimed that, afterward, he was bound to dream of winning the World Cup final.

Christian fell asleep within two minutes of Aunt Eusébie turning out the lights. I was just drifting off when I heard Pacifique's voice. I rushed into the living room, expecting to see him in uniform, but he was dressed in a polo shirt, jeans, and trainers. He lifted me up, holding me at arm's length above his head. "Look at you, my Gaby! You're a man! Soon you'll be taller than your uncle!" He still had the face of an angel and the look of a free-spirited poet, but something in his eyes had changed, he had grown serious. Aunt Eusébie was busy double-locking all the doors with a big set of keys. She returned from the kitchen, flicking off the switch in the living room. A second later, the flame from a cigarette lighter lit a candle on the coffee table, and Pacifique settled into the armchair opposite Maman. She told me to go to bed, adding that the grown-ups needed to talk now. Reluctantly, I turned to leave, but instead of doing as I was told, I stayed in the hallway, just behind the door, where I could watch them unseen.

"Thank you for coming so quickly, big sister," said Pacifique, turning toward Maman once Aunt Eusébie had finally sat down. "I'm sorry that everything's so rushed. The thing is, our wedding couldn't wait. You see, Jeanne's family are devout believers, they're very traditional and like to do things in the right order. So we had to be married before telling them the news, about the baby. Are you following me?" he asked, punctuating his question with a wink.

Maman paused, as if to make sure she had heard properly,

then she let out a whoop of joy and threw her arms around Pacifique. Aunt Eusébie, who was already in on the secret, beamed. Pacifique was quick to pull away from Maman. "Please, sit down," he said, sounding preoccupied. "There's more I need to talk to you about."

His face clouded over. He motioned with his chin to Aunt Eusébie, who immediately went over to the window and glanced outside, after which she closed the blinds and drew the curtains. She returned to sit next to Pacifique, underneath a plastic rococo frame boasting a handsome black-and-white studio photo of her with her husband and children. Oddly, she was the only person smiling in the shot. The rest of the family looked stiff and frozen in front of the camera.

Pacifique pulled up his chair until his knees were touching Maman's. He began to talk in a voice that was almost inaudible.

"Listen carefully, Yvonne. You must take what I'm about to tell you very seriously. The situation is graver than it appears. Our intelligence has intercepted messages that give cause for alarm, and has detected signs that lead us to believe something horrific is about to happen here. The Hutu extremists don't want to power-share with our members in the RPF. They're ready to do whatever it takes to overturn the peace agreements. Their plan is to eliminate all the opposition leaders, as well as every moderate Hutu figure in civil society. Then they'll turn their attention to the Tutsi . . ."

He paused, looking around, straining his ear as he listened out for any untoward noise. Outside, the toads croaked in a regular rhythm. Despite the closed curtains, a pale orange glow from the streetlight had worked its way into the living room.

"We fear widespread slaughters across the country," Pacifique continued, still in a whisper. "Slaughters on a scale that will make what's gone before seem nothing more than a rehearsal."

The candlelight cast shadows on the wall, the darkness blurred my uncle's features so that his eyes appeared suspended in the gloom.

"Machetes have been distributed throughout the provinces, there are significant arms caches in Kigali, the militia are being trained with the support of the regular army, lists of people to be assassinated are being circulated in every district, and the United Nations is in receipt of information confirming that there is the capacity to kill one thousand Tutsis every twenty minutes . . ."

A car drove past outside. Pacifique fell quiet and waited until the vehicle was far enough away.

"There's a long list of what's in store for us," he murmured. "Our families are living on borrowed time. Death is encircling us, soon it will swoop down and there'll be no escape."

Maman's distress and bewilderment were visible as she glanced for confirmation from Aunt Eusébie, who stared bleakly at a spot on the floor.

"What about the Arusha peace agreements?" Maman asked, sounding horrified. "And the transitional government? I thought the war was over, that it was all being resolved. How could a massacre on the scale you're talking about take place in Kigali, in the presence of so many UN peacekeepers? I mean, it's inconceivable . . ."

"All it takes is for a few of those Blue Berets to be killed, and every white in the country will be evacuated. It's part of the Hutu strategy. The powers that be won't risk the lives of their own soldiers on behalf of some poor Africans. And the extremists know that."

"So what are we waiting for? The international press, the

embassies, the United Nations—why haven't they all been informed?"

"Oh, they know what's going on. They can access the same intelligence as us, but they don't place any value on it. We can't expect anything from them. We can only count on ourselves. I've come to see you because we need your help, big sister. I have to make a quick decision, as the only man in our family. I'm asking you to take in Aunt Eusébie's children in Bujumbura, as well as my wife-to-be and the baby she's carrying. They'll stay in Burundi for as long as it takes. They'll be safe over there."

"There's a war being waged in Burundi, too, as well you know."

"What's set to happen here will be far worse than any war."

"When do you plan on sending them?" asked Maman, getting straight to the point.

"Everybody will join you for the Easter holidays, so as not to arouse any suspicions."

"What about you, Eusébie? What are you going to do?"

"I'm staying here, Yvonne, I have to carry on working, for the children's sake. I'll feel less vulnerable without them. In any event, we can't all flee. I'll be all right, don't worry, I have contacts at the United Nations, so if there's a problem I'll make sure I'm evacuated."

We heard the sound of an engine in front of the house. Aunt Eusébie rushed over to the window and parted the curtains slightly. Someone was signaling with their headlights. Then my aunt turned and nodded at Pacifique. When he stood up, I noticed a gun tucked inside the belt of his jeans.

"I have to go now, they're waiting for me. I'll see you tomorrow at the wedding. Drive carefully. I won't be traveling with you to Gitarama: I'm under close surveillance by the secret services and I don't want them making the connection between us. The families of RPF soldiers are at the top of the lists of people to be assassinated. I'll join you when it's time for the ceremony."

Then he slipped outside. I emerged from my hiding place and went over to join my aunt by the window. A motorbike drove off. We could make out the red glow of its rear lights when it braked for potholes. Gradually, the hum of the engine faded until it was out of earshot. Aunt Eusébie closed the curtains again. Nothing moved now. Everything was silent all over the world.

20

THE EARLY-MORNING LIGHT CHASED AWAY THE ANGUISH of the night. I woke to the sounds of laughter as Ana and the cousins played in the garden. Aunt Eusébie and Maman hadn't slept a wink, I'd heard them whispering until dawn. We set out for the wedding straight after breakfast. Christian and I were in the trunk of the car, sitting on the suitcases that contained our outfits. Aunt Eusébie thought it best for us to get dressed on arrival, so as not to draw attention to ourselves in the event of a police check. The girls were wedged together on the backseat. Maman sat in the passenger seat, applying her makeup in the sun-visor mirror. At first, we drove through the poorer districts full of hustle and bustle and tooting horns, then, after the bus station, the landscape gradually became less cluttered. The city gave way to papyrus marshes as far as the eye could see. Gitarama was fifty kilometers from Kigali, and Aunt Eusébie drove fast to reach it as early as possible. We were stuck for ages behind a truck whose exhaust pipe belched out thick, sulphurous black smoke. The girls quickly wound up the windows and pinched their noses at the smell of rotten eggs.

Maman switched on the radio and the catchy rhythm of a Papa Wemba song filled the car. The cousins started moving to the beat, and Christian gave me a mischievous look as he raised his eyebrows and shimmied his shoulders like an Ethiopian dancer. Aunt Eusébie didn't waste any time in turning up the volume. From the back, I had a view of heads swaying left and right to the music. When the chorus came round, the girls sang: "Maria Valencia hey, hey, hey!" This amused Maman, who turned around to give me a knowing wink. The radio presenter was singing over the music. I could grasp only a few words in his Kinyarwanda: "Radio 106 FM! Radio Sympa! Papa Wemba!" Sounding very upbeat, he sang the chorus, chatted, joked, and generally fooled about on air. I got carried away, and even though I usually hate dancing, I found myself wiggling my hips, clapping my hands regardless, and singing enthusiastically "Hey, hey, hey" when, all of a sudden, I noticed that everyone else had stopped moving. The expressions on my cousins' faces had changed. Christian had frozen. Aunt Eusébie hastily switched off the radio. Nobody spoke in the car. Although I couldn't see Maman's face, I could sense her discomfort.

"What is it?" I asked, looking at Christian.

"Nothing. Just some nonsense. It was the radio presenter . . . what he was saying . . ."

"What was he saying?"

"He said all cockroaches must die."

"Cockroaches?"

"Yes, cockroaches. *Inyenzi*."

" . . ."

"They use that word to talk about us, the Tutsi."

The car slowed down. Ahead of us, some vehicles had stopped on a bridge.

"A military roadblock!" said Aunt Eusébie, panicking.

When we were level with the soldiers, one of them signaled to Aunt Eusébie to turn off the engine and then asked to see her identity card. Another, with a Kalashnikov slung across his shoulder, inspected our car, walking around it in a threatening manner. On reaching the trunk, he stuck his face up against the back window. Christian looked away to avoid eye contact, and so did I. The soldier proceeded toward Maman. After staring at her, he asked curtly for her papers. Maman held out her French passport. The soldier glanced at it, then sniggered.

"Bonjour, Madame la Française!"

He leafed through her passport with an amused expression. Maman didn't dare say anything.

"Hmm . . . I don't think you're a *real* Frenchie," he said. "I've never seen a Frenchwoman with a nose like yours. And as for that neck . . ."

He ran his hand down the nape of Maman's neck. She sat there, rigid with fear. Over on her side, Aunt Eusébie was negotiating with the other soldier. She was desperately trying to hide her nervousness.

"We're going to Gitarama to visit a sick relative."

I was staring at the barrier behind the soldiers, at the weapons swinging from their shoulders, and I could hear their straps creaking, as well as the sound of the red-ocher river, squeezed between its papyrus banks, flowing under the bridge with its fleeting eddies on the water's surface. It felt strange to understand the soldier's innuendoes, the fear in Aunt Eusébie's gestures, the fear that had taken hold of Maman. A month earlier, I wouldn't have grasped any of this. But now—Hutu soldiers in one camp, a Tutsi family in the other—I had a ringside seat for this spectacle of hatred.

"Go on, clear off, you bunch of cockroaches!" spat the soldier, flinging Aunt Eusébie's identity card in her face.

The second soldier returned Maman's passport, pushing her nose roughly with the tip of his index finger.

"*Au revoir,* serpentess!" he smirked again. "Oh, and since you're a Frenchie, remember to give a nice deep bow to our friend Tonton Mitterrand!"

When Aunt Eusébie started up the car, one of the soldiers gave the bodywork a kick. With the butt of his gun, the second one smashed a back window, sending shards of broken glass flying over Christian and me. Ana let out a high-pitched shriek. Aunt Eusébie sped off.

WE WERE still in a state of shock when we arrived at Jeanne's house, but Aunt Eusébie asked us not to say anything, for fear of spoiling the celebrations.

Jeanne's family lived in a modest red-brick house, surrounded by a euphorbia hedge, in the hills of Gitarama. Her parents, brothers, and sisters were all waiting for us and we were duly subjected to a lengthy ritual of traditional greetings, by way of a welcome, which included having our backs and arms pummelled while the customary salutations were spoken. Ana and I felt at a loss with our clumsy bodies, and we were incapable of answering the questions our hosts asked us in Kinyarwanda.

Just then, Jeanne appeared in her wedding dress, almost as tall as Pacifique and breathtakingly beautiful. She was holding a bouquet of pink hibiscus flowers, which she gave to Ana. Maman approached her tenderly, cupping the young woman's face in her hands to whisper a few blessings and welcome her into our family.

Once we had changed into our outfits, we headed to the *mairie* on foot. We took a shortcut—a narrow earth track that flanked a series of small village huts all in a row. I was up at the front with Christian, while Jeanne and Maman held each other by the arm as they tried not to lose their footing. The track emerged onto the wide asphalt road leading to Butare. As we trooped along, passersby turned round, bicycles stopped, curious folks came out of their homes to watch us. Their gaze was insistent, boring a hole into us, dissecting us on the spot. Our procession was the talk of the town.

Pacifique was waiting for us in the ceremonial hall, dressed in a gray suit that didn't fit him properly. His gentle and trusting expression had returned. The registrar, on the other hand, appeared to be in a hurry and slightly drunk. For several long, monotonous minutes, he set forth the articles of the law and the duties of the spouses. There weren't many of us in the hall, just close family. Nobody was smiling, some even yawned or stared outside at the tall eucalyptus trees swaying in the sunlight. Pacifique and Jeanne didn't hide their emotions, and seemed to find it funny that they were now husband and wife. They couldn't take their eyes off each other, smiling at their happiness to come, their bodies brushing against one another at every opportunity. They had said yes beneath the portrait of the president. The same one Pacifique had been fighting against before the peace agreements.

After the ceremony, we all walked back to Jeanne's house. The sky was so gray that it was almost dark in the middle of the day and a violent wind whipped up clouds of red dust over the town, ripping the corrugated-iron roofs off some of the huts. Aunt Eusébie told Pacifique that we had to be back in Kigali before the end of the afternoon, it would be safer that way, and he didn't put any pressure on us to stay. He knew the risks and was glad we had made the journey, against the odds.

We were delayed by a sudden downpour that washed the sky and restored the lost sun, and then it really was time to leave. Jeanne thanked us and gave each of us a present. I received a clay statue of a mountain gorilla. Maman wouldn't let go of Jeanne's arm, she kept telling her how impatient she was for Jeanne to join us in Bujumbura so that we could all get to know her properly. When nobody was looking, she slipped a small envelope containing some banknotes into the pocket of Jeanne's elderly father. He thanked her by tipping his funny cowboy hat. Aunt Eusébie wandered with Jeanne down to the bottom of the little garden, where she said a few prayers for the baby and placed her palms on the young bride's belly. Everybody said their goodbyes, surprised to be leaving each other already and taken aback at the speed with which the marriage had been celebrated, almost on the sly. Christian and I clambered back into the trunk.

"We'll throw another party worthy of the name," said Pacifique, leaning into the car after closing Maman's passenger door, "and next time I'll bring my guitar!"

We all voiced our approval.

"Hey, what's happened to your window, Auntie?"

"Oh, nothing, just a little accident."

Aunt Eusébie started up the engine and manoeuvred the car out of the small yard. Before we were through the gates, I turned round to say goodbye. Jeanne and Pacifique were in front, hand in hand in their wedding clothes. Jeanne's father was to one side of them, waving his hat above his head. Behind him, Jeanne's family stood motionless, as if in a painting, with the pinkish late-afternoon light shining sideways on them. The car jolted from left to right, as we made our way slowly back down the dirt track. Eventually they disappeared altogether, swallowed up by the slope.

21

I WAS FINISHING OFF MY HOMEWORK ON A CORNE
the kitchen table while Prothé did the washing up, lost in
thoughts. The radio was broadcasting a speech by the new l
rundian president, Cyprien Ntaryamira, a member of Frodeb
elected by parliament after several months of a power vacuum

That morning, an assassination had taken place in the street
not far from school, and afternoon lessons had been cancelled.
Since my trip to Rwanda and school starting again, I hadn't
been round to see any of my friends. I closed my exercise books
and decided to head over to Gino's, in the hope of ending the
awkwardness that still hovered in the air between us. But he
wasn't at home, so I went to the twins' house instead. They
were slumped on the sofa with Armand, hypnotized by a Kung
Fu film. I stretched out on the living-room rug. The images
paraded in front of me while my mind drifted. I must have
dozed off for a while, because when I opened my eyes again
the credits were slowly rolling. We decided to decamp to the
hideout to play cards. Opening the sliding door of the Combi,
we stumbled on Gino and Francis sharing a cigarette. It took
me a moment to register what I was seeing.

"What's he doing here?" I asked, outraged.

"Calm down. I invited Francis to join our crew. We're going
to need him to protect the street."

Francis was sprawled on the banquette, looking relaxed and at home as he smoked a cigarette from the lit end. Armand and the twins didn't react. So I slammed the door with all my might. I felt betrayed. I was almost out of the patch of wasteland when Gino caught up with me.

"Come back, Gaby! Don't go!"

"What's wrong with you?" I shouted, shoving him backward. "Francis is our bitter enemy and you want him to become part of the group?"

"I didn't know him properly before. I was wrong about him. He's not who you think he is."

"Oh yeah? And what about what he did to us in the river? Have you forgotten that? The maniac wanted to kill us!"

"He's sorry about that, he came knocking at our gate a few days later, to apologize . . ."

"And you believe him? Can't you see it's just another of his ploys? Like at my birthday?"

"No, Gaby, you're wrong. He's on our level. I've talked about a lot of stuff with him. He's really not a bad guy, it's just that he hasn't had much luck in life. He lost his mother, too. Anyway . . . you wouldn't understand, you've still got yours. Losing a mother can make you different sometimes, it toughens you up . . ."

Gino looked down and started scuffing the earth with the toe of his shoe.

"Gino . . . I've been meaning to say . . . I'm sorry, about your mother . . . but how come you never told me?"

"I don't know. See, the thing is, my mother isn't really dead, for me. It's hard to explain. I talk to her, I write her letters, there are even times when I can hear her. D'you understand? My mother's here . . . somewhere . . ."

I wanted to give him a hug, to say something comforting,

but I didn't know how to go about it, or what words to use. I've never known. I felt so close to him, I didn't want to lose Gino: my brother, my friend, my better twin. He was the person I most wanted to be. He possessed the strength and courage I lacked.

"Gino, am I still your best friend?"

He stared me in the eye, before walking over to an acacia bush behind me. He broke off a thorn, sucked it to remove any dust, and then jabbed his fingertip. A drop of blood appeared, like when you do a finger-prick test for malaria. He took one of my fingers and pressed the same thorn into it, until I bled. Then he stuck our two fingers together.

"That's my answer to your question, Gaby. You're my blood brother now. I love you more than anyone."

His voice was wobbly. I had a tickle in my throat. We avoided looking at each other in case either of us started crying. Hand in hand, we made our way back to the Combi.

FRANCIS WAS deep in discussion with the twins and Armand. They were just as transfixed as they had been by the Kung Fu film earlier. He was almost better at storytelling than the twins, punctuating his sentences with made-up words, mixing Swahili, French, English, and Kirundi.

Once the temperature outside began to drop again, we suggested he come with us to cool off in the river.

"If you want to swim, I've got somewhere much better than the Muha," said Francis. "Follow me!"

Out on the main road, he flagged down a blue-and-white taxi. The driver began making excuses, to avoid giving a ride to a bunch of kids, but Francis thrust a one-thousand-franc note under his nose and the guy set off straightaway. We couldn't believe our luck: a magical mystery tour! We were excited to be leaving our street and setting off on an adventure, all of us together.

"Where are we going? Where are we going? Where are we going?" the twins kept asking.

"It's a surprise," Francis replied, enigmatically.

A blast of warm air rushed into the car. Armand was leaning his arm out of the window, his hand an airplane in the wind. The city around us heaved with life, the market area was raucous and the bus station was a tangle of bikes and minibuses. You would never have believed the country was at war. Mango trees laden with fruit adorned the main road, chaussée Prince Louis Rwagasore. Gino tooted the horn when we spotted some kids from another neighborhood picking off mangoes with their long rods. The taxi drove up into the hills surrounding the city, where the air became cooler. We passed the Prince's tomb, with its great cross and three pointed arches in the colors of the national flag. The country's motto was emblazoned above it in capital letters: "Unity Work Progress." We were high enough to glimpse the horizon now. Bujumbura was below us, in the shape of a deckchair by the water's edge. You could have mistaken it for a seaside resort, stretching from the mountain ridge as far as Lake Tanganyika. . . . We stopped in front of the collège du Saint-Esprit, which loomed like a vast ocean liner above the city. We had never been this high up in Bujumbura before. Francis handed another thousand francs to the taxi driver and told him to wait there.

When we entered the school grounds, rain started falling in warm, fat drops that formed tiny craters in the dust and splashed our calves. The scent of damp earth rose up from the ground. Students were running to shelter in their classrooms and dormitories. Soon we were alone in the large empty playground. As we followed Francis along the pathways, I walked with my mouth open to catch the raindrops on my tongue. We discovered the swimming pool behind a low wall. It was like something out of this world. A proper Olympic-sized pool with a high concrete diving platform. In a flash, Francis stripped off and rushed into the pool. Gino followed close on his heels. Then we all undressed, even body-shy Armand, and dive-bombed into the water with our knees against our chests. The rain was beating down in furious squalls onto the water's surface, which was occasionally shot through with a ray of sunshine. We felt as elated as on the first day of falling in love. We laughed like lunatics, tiring ourselves out by swimming lengths and competing in stupid races, tugging each other's legs from below and dunking one another under the water. Francis stood on the pool's edge and performed backflips. Our little gang was under his spell; and Gino more than any of us. All this physical prowess made his eyes shine. I could feel myself gripped by jealousy.

"Wanna dive from the top board?" Gino called out, overcome with admiration.

The rain whipped our faces as Francis stared up at the concrete platform in the sky.

"Hey, you out of your mind? That's like ten meters! I'd kill myself."

I didn't hesitate, not for a second. I wanted to show Gino how much better I was than Francis. I hauled myself out of the water and strode purposefully toward the tall ladder. It was slippery and the top was lost in the mist. Rain was streaming down my face as I climbed, so much so that I couldn't open my eyes. I used all my strength to cling on and prayed that I wouldn't lose my footing. The others were staring at me as if I'd taken leave of my senses. When I reached the top, I walked to the end of the diving board. Down below, the band of brothers watched incredulous, their tiny heads bobbing about like balls in the water. Although I didn't feel dizzy as such, my heart began to race abnormally fast. I wanted to turn back. But I could already picture Francis's reaction, his mean laughter and his sarcasm about spoiled brats wimping out. And Gino would be disappointed, he would close ranks with Francis and turn his back on me, forgetting about our friendship and our blood pact.

From the top of the diving area, I could see Bujumbura, the vast plain and the age-old mountains of Zaire on the other side of the blue expanse that was Lake Tanganyika. I was standing naked above my city and a tropical rain was washing over me, thick as curtains, caressing my skin. Silvery rainbow reflections drifted by in soft clouds. I could hear my friends' voices: "Go on, Gaby! Go, Gaby! Go!" My fear had returned. The same fear that always delighted in paralyzing me. I turned my back to the pool. My heels were hanging over the edge now. Sheer terror made me piss myself, the yellow liquid curling like ivy around my leg. The driving rain pounded like a waterfall, and in the din I let out the whoop of a Sioux chieftain to summon up my courage. Then my legs bent as if they were springs and propelled me backward. My body completed a rotation in the air, in perfect motion, controlled by who knows what mysterious force. Next, I felt myself falling like a ridiculous puppet. I had no idea where I was when the water took me by surprise, welcoming me with cushioning arms, wrapping me like a fever in its eddies and air bubbles. When I reached the bottom of the pool I lay spreadeagled on the tiles, to savor what I'd just accomplished.

And then, on resurfacing, triumph was mine! My friends rushed over shouting: "Gaby! Gaby!" The surface of the water became a drum. Gino raised my arms as if I were a victorious boxer, and Francis kissed my forehead. I could feel their slippery bodies against mine, brushing, gripping, hugging. I'd done it! For the second time in my life, I had overcome my miserable fear. One day I would leave behind that crippling burden.

An elderly caretaker arrived to chase us out of the pool. We gathered up our sodden clothes and ran off, bare-bottomed, laughing until our sides ached. The taxi driver also gave a great belly laugh when he saw us climbing into his cab, in our birthday suits. Night had fallen beneath the rain. Headlights on full beam, the car began its slow descent through the winding roads of Kiriri. In order to see the city below, we had to wipe the steamed-up windows with our underwear. Bujumbura was a plantation of lights now, a field of fireflies illuminating the murky plain. Geoffrey Oryema sang "Makambo" on the radio, his voice a moment of grace, dissolving like sugar in our souls, soothing our excess of happiness. We had never felt so free, so alive from head to toe, all of us as one, joined by the same veins, the same life-force flowing through us. I was sorry for what I'd thought of Francis before. He was like us, like me, just a kid getting by as best he could in a world that didn't give him many choices.

A torrential downpour beat down on Bujumbura. The gutters were overflowing, carrying muddy, rubbish-filled water from the heights of the city all the way down to the lake. The windscreen wipers exhausted themselves, to little effect. In the inky blackness, headlights swept the road, coloring the raindrops yellow and white. We were on our way back to our street, where this crazy afternoon had all begun.

It was on the Muha bridge that the taxi driver suddenly slammed on the brakes. Nobody had been expecting it, and we all crashed into each other as we were flung forward. Francis's head hit the dashboard. When he sat up, there was blood trickling from his nose. As we came to our senses, the taxi driver's physical reaction chilled us to the core. He was petrified.

"*Shetani! Shetani!*" he kept saying, his hands paralyzed on the steering wheel, his terrified gaze on the road. "*Shetani!*" The devil.

Ahead of us, in the darkness, just beyond the beam of the headlights, we saw the shadow of a black horse pass by.

22

ON THE MORNING OF APRIL 7, 1994, THE TELEPHONE
rang and rang. Papa hadn't come home that night. Eventually
I picked up:

"Hello?"

"Hello?"

"Is that you, Maman?"

"Gaby, put your father on the line."

"He isn't here."

"What?"

She stopped short. I could hear the sound of her breathing.

"I'm on my way."

Just as on the day after the coup, there was nobody about
on our land. No Prothé, no Donatien, not even the watchman.
Everyone had vanished. Maman rushed over on her motorbike.
She was still wearing her helmet as she climbed the steps to our
terrace, four at a time, to take Ana and me in her arms. There
was something manic about Maman's gestures. She brewed
some tea in the kitchen and then came to sit down in the living
room. She was holding her cup in both hands, blowing on the
fragrant steam.

"Does your father often leave you alone?"

I blurted out no at the same time as Ana said yes.

"Papa wasn't here on the night of the coup, either." Ana was getting even now.

"Bastard!" exclaimed Maman.

When Papa finally showed up and walked into the living room, he didn't say hello to anybody. But he looked astonished to find Maman sitting on the sofa.

"What are you doing here, Yvonne?"

"Aren't you ashamed of leaving your children alone all night?"

"Okay, I get it . . . So you want to pick a fight? Really? Just remember, you're the one who left the family home, so you're hardly in a position to criticize."

Maman closed her eyes. She stared at the floor and kept sniffing, until she finally wiped her nose on her shirtsleeve. Papa glared at her, ready to do battle. When she looked up, her eyes were red from crying.

"The presidents of Burundi and Rwanda were killed last night," she said. "The plane they were traveling in was shot down over Kigali."

Papa collapsed into a chair. Stunned.

"Jeanne and Pacifique aren't answering the phone. Neither is Aunt Eusébie. I need your help, Michel."

The situation in Bujumbura remained calm, despite the attack and the death of the new president having been announced. Papa contacted the gendarmes at the French embassy while Maman tried desperately to reach her family in Rwanda. Toward the end of the afternoon, Aunt Eusébie finally picked up. Papa listened in on their telephone conversation using the earpiece.

"Yvonne," Aunt Eusébie called out. "Yvonne, is that you? No, things are not okay at all. We heard the airplane exploding yesterday evening. A few minutes later, on the radio, they announced the death of the president, accusing Tutsis of being responsible for the assassination. The Hutu population has been called to take up arms in retaliation. I think it's clear this was their signal to eliminate us. They've wasted no time in setting up roadblocks all over the place. And now the militia and the presidential guard are crisscrossing the city, rounding up people in the different districts, entering the homes of Tutsis and any opposing Hutus, massacring whole families, sparing nobody. Our neighbors and their children were killed this morning, at dawn, right here, on the other side of the fence. It was horrendous, oh my God . . . We witnessed their agony, and there was nothing we could do about it. We're terrified, lying on the floor, inside the house. We can hear machine-gun fire all around us. What on earth can I do, alone with my four children? What's going to happen to us, Yvonne? And my contact at the United Nations isn't answering. I'm not holding out much hope . . ." she faltered.

"Don't say that, Eusébie!" urged Maman, trying to reassure her as best she could. "I'm here with Michel, we'll get through to the French embassy in Kigali. Don't worry. I'm sure Pacifique is already on his way to rescue you. If you can, try to shelter at Sainte-Famille: killers don't attack churches. Remember the pogroms of '63 and '64? That's how we survived, they didn't dare desecrate the sanctuaries . . ."

"It's impossible. The neighborhood is surrounded. I can't risk going outside with the children. I've made up my mind. I'm going to pray with them, then I'll hide them in the false ceiling, and after that I'll go in search of help. But I'd rather say goodbye now. It's better that way. We have little chance of making it, this time. They hate us too much. They want to finish us off once and for all. They've been talking about wiping us out for thirty years. And the time has come for them to execute their plan. There's no pity left in their hearts. We're already dead and buried. We will be the last of the Tutsi. After us, I'm begging you, create a new country. I must leave you now. *Adieu*, my sister, *adieu* . . . Live for us . . . I shall carry your love with me . . ."

When Maman replaced the handset she was terror-stricken, her teeth were chattering and her hands shaking. Papa held her in his arms to soothe her. She quickly recovered her composure and asked Papa to dial another number, then another and another . . .

For days and nights they took it in turns on the telephone, trying to reach the United Nations, as well as the French and Belgian embassies.

"We're only evacuating Westerners," came the cold response on the other end of the line.

"And their dogs and cats, too!" Maman shouted back, enraged.

In the course of the hours, days, and weeks that followed, news reached us from Rwanda that confirmed what Pacifique had predicted a few weeks earlier. Throughout the country, the Tutsi were being systematically and methodically massacred, liquidated, eliminated.

MAMAN HAD stopped eating. She had stopped sleeping. At night, she slipped quietly out of bed. I could hear her picking up the phone in the living room. Dialing the numbers of Jeanne and Aunt Eusébie for the thousandth time. In the morning, I would find her asleep on the sofa, the handset next to her ear, ringing on empty.

Each day, the list of the dead grew longer: Rwanda had become a vast hunting ground in which the Tutsi were the prey.

Human beings guilty of being born, guilty of being. Vermin in the eyes of the killers, cockroaches to be crushed. Maman felt helpless and useless. Despite all her determination and energy, she failed to save a single person. She was a bystander to the disappearance of her people, of her family, and there was nothing she could do about it. She was losing the ground from under her feet and becoming distant from us, as well as from herself, eaten away at from the inside. Her face had aged, heavy shadows outlined her eyes and wrinkles furrowed her brow.

The curtains at home were permanently drawn. We were living in an endless night. The radio reverberated noisily through the large dark rooms, broadcasting distress cries, calls for help and intolerable suffering in the midst of sports results, stock-market news and the kind of minor political stories that keep the world spinning.

In Rwanda, this thing that wasn't war lasted three long months. I can't remember what we did during that period. I have no recollection of school, or my friends, or our daily life. At home, the four of us were back together again, but a giant black hole had swallowed us up, along with our memories. From April to July 1994, at a distance and between four walls, next to a telephone and a radio, we lived through the genocide that was being perpetrated in Rwanda.

The first news reached us at the beginning of June. Pacifique called Mamie's house. He was alive. He had no news of anyone. But he knew that his army, the RPF, was going to seize Gitarama and that he would be at Jeanne's within the week. This information restored a little of our hope. Maman managed to locate some distant relatives and a few friends. Their stories were always terrible and their survival nothing less than a miracle.

The RPF was gaining ground. The Rwandan armed forces

were being pushed back: along with the genocidal government, they had fled the capital. The French army had launched a vast humanitarian operation called "Turquoise" to put a stop to the genocide and secure part of the country. Maman said it was a final dirty trick by France, which was coming to the aid of its Hutu allies.

In July, the RPF finally arrived in Kigali. Maman, Mamie, and Rosalie left immediately for Rwanda, in search of Aunt Eusébie, her children, Jeanne, Pacifique, our family, and friends. Three generations were returning to their country after thirty years of exile. They had dreamed about this return, especially old Rosalie. She wanted to end her days in the land of her ancestors. But the Rwanda of milk and honey had disappeared. It was now a mass grave, open to the skies.

23

THE SCHOOL YEAR WAS APPROACHING ITS END. IN Bujumbura, the first departures linked to the country's political situation were underway. The twins' father had decided to return to France, for good: the news dropped like a guillotine blade, from one day to the next. We said our goodbyes in front of the gates to their house, and their car sped off in a cloud of dust. It all happened too fast, so Francis had the idea of taking a taxi to the airport. We arrived just before the twins were due to board. We hugged each other. I made them promise to write to me. They swore they would, "In God's name!"

The twins left a void behind them. The first few times we met up in the Combi, on our patch of wasteland, the laughter was missing from Armand's jokes and from our afternoon stories. More than anything, the twins' departure made more space for Francis. From then on, all we did was talk. We would sit for hours on the Combi's banquette, listening to an old Peter Tosh cassette, smoking cheap cigarettes, and necking beers and Fantas that Francis bought us at the kiosk. Whenever I suggested going fishing, or a river trip or mango-picking, everyone told me to get lost: they were kids' games and we were too old for them now.

"Gotta find ourselves a proper name," said Gino.

"We already have one! The Kinanira Boyz."

"Pathetic!" sneered Gino and Francis.

"You came up with it, Gino," I pointed out, feeling aggrieved.

"Look, whatever, we're done with 'crews' and 'bands of brothers,'" said Francis. "What we're talking about now is a gang. Buja is a city of gangs, like Los Angeles or New York. There's one for every 'hood. In Bwiza, it's 'The Diehards,' in Ngagara it's 'The Invincibles,' in Buyenzi it's 'The Six Garages...'"

"Yeah, yeah, and there's the 'Chicago Bulls' and the 'Raw Dogs,'" said Gino, like he was starting to rap.

"We're going to be the gang for Kinanira," said Francis, taking a drag on his cigarette. "Let me explain how it works. Gangs are armed and they have structures, with a hierarchy and everything. They man the roadblocks during lockdowns. Everyone respects them. Even the soldiers leave them alone."

"Yeah, but we won't be taking part in lockdowns, right, guys?" asked Armand.

"Gotta protect the, 'hood," replied Gino.

"Listen up, my friend, with a dad like mine," Armand grinned, "if I go out during lockdown it won't just be the city that gets locked down."

"Chill out, we won't man the roadblocks straightaway," said Francis, who was clearly starting to think of himself as our leader. "I just want us to be on good terms with 'The Invincibles' who block the Muha bridge. Gotta show them we're with them, lend them a hand from time to time—that way we can move around the 'hood without any hassle, and they'll protect us if we need it."

"I don't want anything to do with those murderers," I pointed out. "The only thing they know about is killing poor houseboys on their way home from work."

"They kill Hutus, Gaby, and the Hutu kill us!" replied

Gino. "An eye for an eye, a tooth for a tooth, get it? It's even in the Bible."

"Bible? Never heard of it! But I know that Ndombolo song: '*Eye for an eye, Blood for a blud! Hundred percent! Oh! Oh! Oh!*'"

"Stop it, Armand!" I objected. "There's nothing funny about this."

"Have you seen what they've done to our families in Rwanda, Gaby?" Gino went on. "If we don't protect ourselves, they'll kill us, just like they killed my mother."

Francis was blowing smoke-rings above our heads. Armand stopped clowning about. I wanted to tell Gino that he was mistaken, that he was making generalizations, that if we took revenge every time, then the war would never end, but I was caught off-guard because he had just revealed the truth about his mother. His grief outweighed his reason, I told myself. Suffering is a wildcard in the game of debate, it wipes the floor with all other arguments. Looked at one way, it has an unfair advantage.

"Gino's right. Nobody can be neutral in war!" said Francis, with that know-it-all way of his that got right up my nose.

"You can talk, you're from Zaire!" Armand burst out laughing.

"Yeah, I'm from Zaire, but I'm a Zairean Tutsi."

"Get that, you learn something new every day!"

"They call us the Banyamulenge."

"Never heard of them," said Armand.

"What if we don't want to choose a side?" I asked.

"You don't have a choice, everyone belongs to one camp or the other," said Gino, with a hostile grin.

I was bored by these discussions and by the violence that seemed to fascinate Francis and Gino. I made up my mind not to visit the hideout so often. I even started avoiding my friends with their war obsession. I needed to breathe, to take a break. For the first time in my life I felt suffocated by our dead-end street, where my worries went round in circles.

ONE AFTERNOON, I ran into Madame Economopoulos in front of her bougainvillea hedge. We exchanged a few words about the tropical weather, and before I knew it she had invited me into her house for a glass of barbadine juice. In her grand salon my gaze was immediately drawn to her wood-paneled library, whose shelves lined one of the walls. I'd never seen so many books in one place. Floor to ceiling.

"Have you read all those books?" I asked her.

"Yes. I've even read some of them many times over. They're the great loves of my life. They make me laugh and weep and question and reflect on things. They allow me to escape from myself. They've changed me, they've made me a different person."

"A book can change us?"

"Of course a book can change you. It can even change your life. It's like falling in love. And you never know when such an encounter might happen. You should beware of books, they're sleeping genies."

I ran my fingers along the shelves, stroking the different textures of those spines. Silently, I mouthed the names of the titles. Madame Economopoulos watched me without saying anything, but when I hovered over one particular book, intrigued by its title, she encouraged me.

"Take it, I'm sure you'll enjoy it."

That evening, before going to bed, I borrowed a torch from one of the drawers in Papa's writing desk. Under the sheets, I began to read the novel: it was the story of an old fisherman, a small boy, a large fish, and a shiver of sharks. While I read, my bed was transformed into a boat, I could hear the waves splashing against my mattress, I could smell the air of the open sea and feel the wind blowing into the sails of my sheets.

The next day, I returned the book to Madame Economopoulos.

"Have you finished it already? *Bravo*, Gabriel! I shall lend you another one."

The following night, I heard swords clashing, horses galloping, the swish of chevaliers' capes, the rustle of a princess's lace dress.

Another day, I was in a cramped room with a teenage girl and her family, in a ruined wartime city. Over her shoulder, she let me read the thoughts she was inscribing in her diary. She wrote about her fears, her dreams, her loves, and her life before. I felt as if she could have been writing about me, as if I could have written those lines.

Each time I returned a book, Madame Economopoulos wanted to know what I'd thought of it. I wondered why it mattered to her. At first, I would give her a brief outline of the story, as well as listing a few important events, the names of the places and protagonists. I could see that she enjoyed this and, above all, I wanted to be sure that she would lend me another book, so that I could disappear into my bedroom and devour it.

But as time went on, I started to tell her about how the book had made me feel, about the questions it had prompted me to ask, and about my opinion of the author and the characters. It was my way of savoring the book and prolonging the story. I fell into the habit of visiting her every afternoon. Thanks to my reading, I had broken free from the limits of our street and was able to breathe again; the world seemed bigger now, extending beyond the fences that encouraged us to turn in on ourselves, huddled up with our fears. I didn't go to the hide-out anymore, I didn't want to see my friends or listen to them talking about the war, lockdowns, Hutus, and Tutsis. Instead, I would sit with Madame Economopoulos in her garden, beneath a jacaranda tree. She served tea and warm biscuits at her wrought-iron table. For hours at a time we discussed the books that she pressed into my hands. I discovered that I could talk about all sorts of things buried inside me that I'd been unaware of before. In that haven of greenery I learned to express my tastes, my desires, my way of seeing and responding to the world. Madame Economopoulos made me more confident in myself, she never judged me and she had a gift for listening and reassuring me. After we had talked about a book at length, and just as the afternoon was disappearing with the setting sun, we would stroll through her garden like a pair of unlikely lovers. I felt as if we were walking beneath the vaulting of a church, and the birdsong was a murmuring of prayers. We lingered in front of the wild orchids, or edged our way between the hibiscus hedges and the aerial roots of the rubber fig tree. Madame Economopoulos's flowerbeds were sumptuous feasts for the sunbirds as well as for the neighborhood bees. I collected dried leaves from under the trees to make into bookmarks. We walked at our leisure, almost in slow motion, allowing our feet to trail through the plump grass as if to hold back time, while, out on our street, little by little, night fell.

24

MAMAN RETURNED FROM RWANDA ON THE DAY TERM
started again. It was just after a lockdown. The route to school
was littered with burned-out cars, blocks of stone obstructing
our way, and melted tires, some of which were still steaming.
Whenever there was a body by the side of the road, Papa ordered us not to look.

The principal of our school, accompanied by gendarmes
from the French embassy, assembled everyone in the main
playground to update us on the new security measures. The
bougainvillea bushes surrounding the school had been replaced
with a high brick wall to keep out the stray bullets, which
sometimes lodged themselves in the classrooms.

A sense of intense anxiety descended on the city. The
grown-ups were afraid that new dangers were just around the
corner. They worried the situation would deteriorate, just as it
had in Rwanda. And so, increasingly, we barricaded ourselves
in, as the season of violence led to a boom in metal fencing,
guards, alarms, barriers, security metal detectors, and barbed
wire: all the reassuring paraphernalia to persuade us we could
push back the violence, keep it at bay. We were living in a limbo
that was neither peace nor war. The values we had grown up
with no longer held sway. Feeling unsafe was as commonplace

as hunger, thirst, or heat. Blood and fury rubbed shoulders with our everyday actions.

One day, during rush hour, I witnessed the lynching of a man in front of the central post office. Papa was in the car, having sent me to collect the mail from our PO box. I was keeping my fingers crossed for some news from Laure. Just then, three young guys walked in front of me and suddenly attacked a man, for no apparent reason. They stoned him. Two police officers watched the scene without moving from their corner of the street. Passersby paused for a moment, taking advantage of the free entertainment. One of the three attackers went to fetch a huge block of stone from under a frangipani, where the cigarette and chewing-gum sellers usually sat. Just as the victim was struggling to his feet, the boulder came crashing down on his head. His body crumpled onto the tarmac. His chest rose three times under his shirt, in rapid succession. He was searching for air. Then nothing. The attackers left, as calmly as they had arrived, and the passersby went on their way, avoiding the corpse much as they might have walked around a traffic cone. The entire city was bustling, going about its business, shopping and continuing with its daily grind. Traffic was heavy, minibuses blasted their horns, street vendors touted bags of water and peanuts, there were sweethearts hoping to find love letters in their PO boxes, a child bought white roses for his sick mother, a woman sold tins of tomato concentrate, a teenager emerged from the barber's with the latest style and, for some time now, men had been able to kill other men with absolute impunity, under the same midday sun as before.

WE WERE sitting around our table when Jacques's car pulled up at the house. Maman stepped out of the Range Rover. It had been two months since we'd last had any news from her. She was unrecognizable. Emaciated. A *pagne* was crudely tied around her waist, a brownish shirt swamped her upper body and her bare feet were coated in filth. She was no longer the young, elegant, sophisticated city-dweller that we knew: she looked like a mud-caked peasant returning from her field of beans. Ana bounded down the steps and threw herself into her arms, but Maman was so unsteady she nearly keeled over backward.

I saw how gaunt she had become, there were dark rings around her yellowed eyes and her skin was withered. Her open shirt collar revealed discolored patches on her body. She had grown old.

"I found Yvonne in Bukavu," said Jacques. "I was on my way to Buja and I came across her by chance, on the outskirts of the city."

Jacques didn't dare look at Maman. It was as if she disgusted him. He kept on talking to offload his sense of embarrassment, while pouring himself glass after glass of whiskey. The heat was causing large drops of sweat to form on his brow. He mopped his face repeatedly with a thick handkerchief.

"Bukavu is a goddamn shambles at the best of times, but you wouldn't believe your eyes now, Michel, it's beyond the unthinkable. A human dumping ground. Market stalls of misery every square centimeter. A hundred thousand refugees in the streets. Total gridlock. Not a scrap of pavement left. And the flow of human traffic continues, they arrive in their thousands every day. It's a mass exodus. Rwanda is bleeding into us: two million women, children, old people, goats, and Interahamwe, and then, alongside those Hutu paramilitaries, come the officers of the former Rwandan army, as well as ministers, bankers, priests, cripples, the innocent, the guilty, and I'm leaving plenty out here . . . There's everything humanity has to offer, from ordinary people to the big bastards. They've left behind scavenging dogs, amputated cows, and a million dead on the hillside, to come to our country and help themselves to famine and cholera. You've got to wonder how the Kivu region will get back on its feet after this God-awful fuck-up!"

Prothé was serving Maman beef with potato purée, when Ana asked the question that had been troubling all of us:

"Did you find Auntie Eusébie and the cousins?"

Maman shook her head. We were waiting for her answer, but she said nothing. I wanted to ask the same question about Pacifique, but Papa signaled to me to wait a while. Maman chewed her food slowly, like a sick old man. With weary movements, she picked up her glass of water and took small sips. She kneaded the soft part of the bread and rolled it into tiny balls, which she placed methodically in front of her plate. She didn't look at us, she was concentrating on the food. When she belched noisily, we all stopped to stare at her, even Prothé, who was beginning to clear the table. She carried on as if nothing had happened, taking another sip of water and then swallowing a morsel of bread. This behavior, this demeanor . . . it couldn't be her . . . Papa wanted to make some kind of contact, but didn't know how to without rushing her. In the end, Maman spoke of her own accord, in a slow, calm voice, the way she used to tell me stories to lull me to sleep when I was a little boy:

"I reached Kigali on the fifth of July. The city had just been liberated by the RPF. All along the road, a never-ending line of corpses littered the ground. I could hear sporadic gunfire. The RPF soldiers were killing hordes of dogs that had been feeding on human flesh for three months. Survivors with dazed eyes roamed the streets. I arrived in front of Aunt Eusébie's gate.

It was open. When I stepped onto her land, I wanted to turn back because of the smell. Somehow, I found the courage to go on. In the living room there were three children on the floor. I came across the fourth body, Christian, in the hallway. I recognized him from the Cameroonian football shirt he was wearing. I searched everywhere for Aunt Eusébie. No sign. And nobody could help me. I was alone. I had to bury the children in the garden by myself. I stayed in that house for a week. I kept thinking that Aunt Eusébie would come home eventually. When she still didn't return, I decided to set off in search of Pacifique. I knew that his first instinct would be to go to Gitarama to find Jeanne. I reached her house to discover that it had been looted, but there was no sign of Jeanne or her family. The next day, an RPF soldier informed me that Pacifique was in prison. They wouldn't let me see him when I arrived there. I went back for three consecutive days. On the morning of the fourth day, one of the wardens led me behind the prison, to a football pitch, on the edge of a banana plantation. Some RPF soldiers were keeping guard. Pacifique was sprawled on the grass. He had just been shot. The warden told me how, when he'd got to Gitarama, Pacifique had discovered that his entire family-in-law, together with his wife, had been murdered in their backyard. Some Tutsi neighbors, who had escaped the massacre, accused a group of Hutus, still in town, of committing the crime. Pacifique found them in the main square. One of the men in the group was wearing Jeanne's father's hat. A woman wore the flowery dress Pacifique had given Jeanne for their engagement. My brother felt himself come undone. He emptied his gun into those four people. He was immediately court-martialed and condemned to death. When I tracked down Mamie and Rosalie in Butare, I lied to them. I said that Pacifique had fallen in battle, for the country, for us, for our return. They could never have accepted the idea that he had been killed by his own. An acquaintance, who had made her way back from Zaire, told us she thought she'd spotted Aunt Eusébie in a camp, toward Bukavu. So I took to the road again and spent a month trying to find her. I kept walking, farther and farther. I wandered into refugee camps. I was nearly killed dozens of times when they guessed that I was Tutsi. By some miracle, Jacques recognized me by the roadside, when I had lost all hope of finding Aunt Eusébie."

Maman fell quiet. Papa's eyes were closed, his head flung backward, and Ana was sobbing in his arms.

"Africa, what a waste!" cursed Jacques, pouring himself another stiff glass of whiskey.

I ran to shut myself in my bedroom.

25

I HAD A CHIGOE FLEA IN THE SOLE OF MY FOOT, FROM walking outside without shoes. Prothé brought over a small stool and rested my heel on it, while Donatien used a lighter to burn the end of a needle.

"You're not going to cry, are you, Gaby?" asked Donatien.

"Oh no, Monsieur Gabriel is a man, now!" Prothé teased kind-heartedly.

"Be gentle, Donatien!" I yelped, as Papa's foreman approached with the glowing red needle.

He removed the larva at the first go. The pain was bad, but bearable.

"Will you look at the size of this grub? I'm going to disinfect the wound and, after that, you must promise me not to walk around barefoot anymore. Not even in the house!"

Donatien dabbed my foot with antiseptic and Prothé checked that I didn't have any more parasites. I watched these two men taking care of me as tenderly as if they were my mother. The war was ravaging their neighborhood, but they came to work almost every day and their fear and dread never showed.

"Is it true that the army has killed people where you live, in Kamenge?" I asked.

Donatien lowered my foot carefully onto the stool. Prothé

came over to sit next to him, folding his arms as he watched the black kites circling in the sky.

"Yes, that is what's happening," Donatien began, sounding tired. "Kamenge is the seat of all the violence in this city. Every night, we go to sleep on burning embers and we see flames rising above the country, flames so high they mask the stars we loved to gaze on. And when morning comes, we're surprised to find that we're still here, that we can hear the cockerel crowing and see the light on the hills. I wasn't a fully-grown man when I left the Zaire of my parents and fled our wretched village. I found a corner of paradise in Bujumbura, the city that became my own. I lived my best years in Kamenge, without realizing it, because I was always thinking about the next day, hoping that tomorrow would be better than yesterday. Happiness is something you only see in the rear-view mirror. The next day? Look at it. Here it is. Slaughtering hope, making the horizon futile, crushing dreams. I prayed for us, Gaby, I prayed as often as I could. The more I prayed, the more God abandoned us, and the more faith I had in his strength. God makes us undergo these ordeals so we can prove to him that we don't doubt him. It's as if he's telling us that great love relies on trust. We shouldn't doubt the beauty of things, not even under a torturing sky. If you aren't surprised by the cockerel's crow or the light above the mountain ridge, if you don't believe in the goodness of your soul, then you're not striving anymore, and it's as if you were already dead."

"Tomorrow, the sun will rise and we shall try again," Prothé concluded.

All three of us fell silent, lost in our somber thoughts, at which point Gino appeared.

"Gaby, get over here! There's something I have to show you."

My best friend was agitated. He pulled me off my stool and started running ahead of me. I hobbled along behind him, no questions asked. I made my way up our street as fast as I could, arriving at his house completely out of breath. Francis and Armand were sitting at the kitchen table. Gino walked over to the fridge. From the living room, we could hear the clickety-clack of his father's typewriter.

"Right, now you've got to open the freezer," Gino told us, looking at Armand and me.

Francis was clearly in on the game: his knowing glance to Gino made me fear the worst. Armand tugged on the freezer handle. Not realizing what it was at first, I picked up one of two objects.

"Shit! A grenade!"

I immediately put it down again, closing the door and retreating to the back of the room.

"Guess how much we got both grenades for?" said Gino, too excited to wait for our answer. "Five thousand! Francis knew the guy from 'The Invincibles.' He explained that we were taking care of Kinanira, and he cut us a deal. Normally, it's twice as expensive."

"Holy shit, Gino, you've got fucking grenades in your fridge!" said Armand. "Are you out of your mind?"

"What's your problem?" asked Francis, seizing him by the collar.

"You lot are insane!" Armand panicked. "You've gone and bought grenades, you're storing them next to a fillet of frozen beef, and you're asking *me* if I've got a problem?"

"Shut it, Armand, my father might hear us. Let's go to the hideout."

Gino took the grenades out of the freezer, stuffed them into a plastic bag, and we trooped off to the Combi. Once we were inside the wreck, Francis removed both explosives from the bag, to hide them in the storage space under the rear banquette. When I lifted up the seat, I spotted a telescope.

"What's that doing here?" I asked him.

"I've got a buyer. With the money we make on this, we'll be able to save up for a Kalashnikov. You can get them second-hand from Jabe market."

"A Kalashnikov?" said Armand. "Why not an Iranian atomic bomb, while we're at it?"

"I recognize that telescope, it belongs to Madame Economopoulos. Did you steal it from her?"

"Don't give us grief, Gaby," said Francis. "Nobody gives a shit about that old cow. She won't even notice it's missing, with all that junk she's got piled up at her place."

"You have to give it back to her straightaway!" I said. "She's a friend, and I don't want you stealing from her."

"Spare us the guilt trip," said Gino. "You were happy enough to steal mangoes from her garden and then sell them back to her. You conned the Greek lady, too."

"That was before! And anyway, it's not the same with mangoes . . ."

I tried to grab hold of the telescope, but Gino pushed me backward. When I lunged for him again, Francis caught me from behind and got me in a hammerlock.

"Let me go! I don't want to hang out with you guys anymore. What's happened to you, Gino? I don't recognize you these days. D'you have any idea what you're doing? Or what you're turning into?"

My voice was trembling and I was crying with anger.

"Gaby, this is war," said Gino, sounding exasperated. "We're protecting our street, because if we don't, they'll kill us. When are you going to understand? What world are you living in?"

"We're just a bunch of kids. Nobody's asking us to fight, or steal, or have enemies."

"Our enemies are already here. They're called the Hutu and those savages won't think twice about killing a bunch of kids. Look what they did to your cousins, in Rwanda. We're not safe. We've got to learn how to defend ourselves and fight back. What are you going to do when they enter our street? Offer them mangoes?"

"I'm neither Hutu nor Tutsi," I replied. "Those are not my stories. You're my friends because I love you, not because you're from one ethnic group or another. I don't want anything to do with all that!"

While we were arguing, far off, up in the hills, we could hear the AMX-10 tanks firing. Over time, I had learned to recognize their notes in the musical stave of war that surrounded us. There were evenings when the noise of weapons blended into the birdsong or the call of the muezzin, and I found such beauty in this peculiar soundscape that I forgot myself entirely.

26

MAMAN HAD BEEN LIVING WITH US SINCE HER RETURN. She slept in our bedroom, on a mattress at the foot of my bed, and spent her days on the covered terrace with a faraway look in her eyes. She didn't want to see anybody and wasn't strong enough to go back to work. Papa said she needed time to recover from everything she'd been through.

She rose late. We heard the water running in the bathroom for hours. Then she would make her way over to the sofa on the *barza* and sit there, motionless, staring at a nest of potter wasps in the ceiling. If one of us passed by, she would ask for a beer, but she refused to eat meals with us. Ana would prepare her a plate, which she placed on a stool in front of her. Maman didn't eat, she picked at her food. Come nightfall, she remained on the terrace, alone in the dark. She went to bed late, after we had already been asleep for some time. I learned to accept her condition when I stopped searching for the mother I had known before. Genocide is an oil slick: those who don't drown in it are polluted for life.

Sometimes, arriving back from Madame Economopoulos's house with a pile of books under my arm, I would sit next to Maman and read to her. I tried to find stories that weren't too cheerful, so as not to remind her of the good life we had lost, but I didn't want them to be too sad, either, and risk stirring up her grief, that swamp of unspeakable things festering inside her. When I closed my book, she would glance absently in my direction. I had become a stranger to her, and I would flee the terrace, terrified by the emptiness in her eyes.

Late one night, as she was coming into our bedroom, she banged her foot against a chair and I woke up. I saw her shadow staggering in the dark. She was groping her way toward Ana's side of the room. Once she was by my sister's bedside, she leaned over and whispered: "Ana?"

"Yes, Maman."

"Are you asleep, my darling?"

"Yes, I was asleep . . ."

Maman's voice was thick as an old soak's.

"I love you, my baby, you know that?"

"Yes, Maman. I love you, too."

"I thought about you, when I was over there. I thought about you so much, my little sweetheart."

"Me too, Maman, I thought about you."

"And your cousins, did you think about them? Those kind girls you used to have such fun with?"

"Yes, I thought about them."

"That's good, that's good . . ."

Then, after a short silence:

"Do you remember your cousins?"

"Yes."

"When I arrived at Auntie Eusébie's house, they were the ones I saw first. Lying on the living-room floor. For three months. D'you know what a body looks like, after three months, my baby?"

" . . ."

"It looks like nothing at all. Except rottenness. I wanted to hold them in my arms, but I couldn't, they trickled through my fingers. I gathered them up. Piece by piece. They're in the garden now, where you used to enjoy playing. Underneath the tree, the one with the swing. Do you remember? Answer me. Tell me you remember. Tell me."

"Yes, I remember."

"But in the house there were still those four stains on the floor. Huge stains where they had lain for three months. I scrubbed and scrubbed and scrubbed with water and a sponge. But the stains wouldn't go. There wasn't enough water. I had to find some in the neighborhood. So I searched in the houses. I should never have gone inside those houses. There are some things you should never see in your lifetime. But that's what I had to do, to get some water. Once I'd finally managed to fill a bucket, I went back and carried on scrubbing. I scraped the ground with my nails, but their skin and blood had soaked into the cement. Their smell clung to me. A smell that will never leave me. No matter how much I wash myself, I am dirty, I smell of their death, still. And those three stains in the living room were Christelle, Christiane, and Christine. And the stain in the hall was Christian. And I had to remove all traces of them before Aunt Eusébie returned. Because you have to understand, my poppet, a mother mustn't see the blood of her children in her own house. So I scrubbed, I scrubbed those stains that will never go. They stayed there, in the cement, in the stone, they stayed . . . I love you, my treasure . . ."

And, leaning over Ana, Maman carried on narrating her dreadful story in a long breathless whisper. I pulled my pillow over my head. I didn't want to know. I didn't want to hear anything. I wanted to curl up inside a mouse-hole, hide away in a den, protect myself from the world beyond our street, I wanted to lose myself in happy memories, to be inhabited by gentle novels, to live deep inside books.

THE NEXT morning, the first rays of sunlight knocked at the windows. It wasn't yet six o'clock and the heat was already overwhelming. A heavy thunderstorm was brewing. I opened my eyes, Maman was breathing noisily, stretched out on Ana's mattress, her feet hanging off the end of the bed, still dressed in her washed-out *pagne* and brownish shirt. I shook my sister to wake her up. She was exhausted. The two of us struggled to get ready in silence. I pretended I hadn't heard anything the night before. Maman was still asleep when Papa drove us to school.

I came home to find her on the *barza*, gazing in the direction of the wasps' nest. Her eyes were red and her hair disheveled. Bubbles rose in her glass of beer on the stool opposite. I greeted her without waiting for a reply.

We ate supper earlier than usual. The sky was threatening, the air saturated with humidity, and the heat unbearable. Papa and I were shirtless. I was squishing mosquitoes against my soup bowl: they were gorged on blood. We could hear bats flying over the house. They were leaving the kapok trees in the city center for a night raid on the papaya trees by the shores of Lake Tanganyika. Ana kept nodding off, unable to keep her eyes open, exhausted by her broken night. Beyond the glass door of the living room, in the darkness, I could see Maman's mournful figure, so still, on the terrace sofa.

"Gaby, go and turn on the outside light," instructed Papa. The small signs of kindness he showed Maman were a comfort to me. He still loved her. I pressed the switch, the light blinked several times, and then Maman's face appeared. Expressionless.

The storm broke in the night, torrential rain drumming on the corrugated roof. The cracked road in our *impasse* was transformed into a giant pond. Water engulfed the rivulets and gutters. Lightning streaked the sky and lit up our room, tracing Maman's silhouette over Ana's bed. She had woken her up to tell her the story of the stains on the ground all over again. Her voice was frightening. Hollow. The stench of alcohol on her breath traveled across the room, reaching me. When Ana didn't answer her questions, Maman shook her violently before apologizing and babbling sweet nothings into her ear. Outside, an army of flying termites bustled hysterically around the white neon lights.

We're alive. They're dead. Maman couldn't abide this idea. She wasn't as crazy as the world that surrounded us. I didn't hold it against her, but I was afraid for Ana. Every night, from then on, Maman insisted on exploring the land of nightmares with her daughter. I had to rescue Ana, to rescue us. I wanted Maman gone, for her to leave us in peace, to spare us from the horrors she had experienced so that we could still dream and hold out hope in life. I didn't understand why we had to suffer with her.

I went to find Papa to tell him what had been happening. I lied, exaggerating Maman's brutality to make him react. When he confronted her about it, he was uncompromising and ferocious. The argument deteriorated as Maman rediscovered the kind of vigor we thought had disappeared. She was transformed into a fury, foaming at the mouth, her eyes bulging. She ranted and raved, insulting us in every language, accusing the French of being responsible for the genocide. She lunged at Ana, grabbing her by the arms and shaking her like a palm tree.

"You don't love your mother! You prefer these two Frenchmen, your family's murderers!"

Papa tried to rescue Ana from Maman's clutches. My sister

was traumatized. Maman's nails were digging into her flesh, tearing at her skin.

"Help me, Gaby!" Papa called out.

I couldn't move, I was rooted to the spot. One by one, Papa prized apart Maman's fingers. But no sooner had he succeeded in making her let go than she spun round, seized an ashtray from the coffee table, and hurled it at Ana's face. There was a gash above my sister's eyes, with blood oozing from it. Everything seemed disjointed and momentarily suspended in time. Then Papa carried Ana out to the car and rushed her straight to hospital. I escaped to the Combi and waited for darkness to fall, before venturing back into the house. By the time I returned, Maman had vanished into the night. Papa and Jacques spent whole days scouring the city for her, telephoning her family, her friends, the hospitals, the police stations, the morgues. To no avail. I felt guilty for wishing her gone. I was a coward, as well as being selfish. I wanted to make a fortress of my happiness and a chapel of my innocence. I wanted life to leave me intact, whereas Maman, risking her own life, had sought out her relatives at the gates of hell. She would have done the same for Ana and me, without a second's hesitation. I knew that. I loved her. And now that she had disappeared with her wounds, she left us nursing ours.

27

Dear Christian,

I waited for you during the Easter holidays. Your bed was made up, next to mine. I'd pinned up a few pictures of footballers above it. I'd made some room in my wardrobe, so you could keep your clothes and ball in there. I was ready to welcome you.

You're not coming.

There are lots of things I never had time to tell you about. Take Laure, for instance, I realize I never told you about her. She's my fiancée. She doesn't know it yet, but I'm planning on asking her to marry me. Very soon. Once peace is here. Laure and I talk to each other with letters. Letters sent by airplane. Paper-storks flying between Africa and Europe. It's the first time I've fallen in love with a girl. It's a funny feeling. Like a fever in your belly. I don't dare tell my friends about it, they'd only make fun of me. They'd say I'm in love with a ghost. Because I haven't even seen this girl yet. But I don't need to meet her to know I love her. Our letters are enough for me.

It's taken me a long time to write to you. I've been very busy recently, trying to stay a child. I'm worried about my friends. They're drifting further away from me every day.

They argue about stuff that's meant for grown-ups, they invent enemies and reasons for fighting. My father was right to stop Ana and me from getting mixed up in politics. Papa looks tired. He seems absent. Distant. He's built up some heavy armor for himself, so the evil glances off him. But I know that deep down he's as soft as the pulp of a ripe guava.

Maman never returned from visiting you. She left her spirit in your garden. Her heart is cracked. She has grown mad, like the world that took you away.

It's taken me a long time to write to you. I was listening to a host of voices telling me so many different things . . . My radio told me that the Nigerian football team—the one you were supporting—won the Africa Cup of Nations. My great-grandmother told me that the people we love don't die as long as we keep thinking about them. My father told me that on the day men stop waging war on one another, it will snow over the tropics. Madame Economopoulos told me that words hold more truth than reality. My biology teacher told me that the earth is round. My friends told me that we have to choose which side we're on. My mother told me that you're sleeping for a long time, wearing the football shirt of your favorite team.

But you, Christian, you won't tell me anything ever again.

    Gaby

28

SPRAWLED ON THE TILED FLOOR OF THE TERRACE,
with her felt-tip pens and coloring pencils scattered around her,
Ana was drawing cities on fire, armed soldiers, blood-splattered
machetes, torn flags. The smell of crepes filled the air. Prothé
was cooking with the radio on full blast. The dog was sleeping
peacefully at my feet. He woke from time to time, to chew his
paw in a frenzy. Blow flies buzzed around his muzzle. Sitting
in Maman's favorite spot on the terrace, I was reading *The Boy
and the River* by Henri Bosco, lent to me by Madame Economopoulos. I heard the metal chain on the gates coming loose.
I rose to my feet to see five men heading up the path. One of
them had a Kalashnikov. He was the one who told us to come
out of the house. He gave his orders from behind his gun. Prothé raised his arms in the air, and Ana and I copied him. The
men made us kneel down with our hands behind our heads.

"Where's the boss?" asked the man with the Kalashnikov.

"He's traveling in the north of the country for a few days,"
said Prothé.

The men stared at us. They were young, and some of them
looked familiar: I had probably seen them at the kiosk.

"You, Hutu, where d'you live?" the man went on, address-
ing Prothé.

"I've been living here for the past month," said Prothé. "I

sent my family back to Zaire, because of the violence. I sleep over there now," he added, pointing to the small metal hut at the bottom of the garden.

"We don't want any Hutus in the neighborhood," said the man with the Kalashnikov. "Get it? We'll let you lot work here in the daytime, but at night you go back home."

"I can't go back to my district, Chief, my house has been burned down."

"Don't complain. You're lucky to be alive. Your boss is French and, like all French, he prefers Hutus. But this is not Rwanda, and they're not going to lay down the law here. We're the ones who decide."

He walked over to Prothé and pushed the barrel of his weapon into our cook's mouth.

"So by the end of the week, either you clear out, or we'll take care of you. As for you two, make sure you tell your father we don't want any Frenchies in Burundi. You've killed us off in Rwanda."

Before removing his weapon from Prothé's mouth, the man spat on him. Then he signaled to the rest of the group with a jerk of his head and they left. We waited a long time before getting to our feet. Afterward, we sat on the steps of the house. Prothé didn't say anything. He looked crushed, staring at the floor. Ana started drawing again, as if nothing had happened.

"Gaby," she asked eventually, looking up at me, "why did Maman accuse us of having killed our family in Rwanda?"

I had no answer to give my little sister. I had no explanation for the deaths of some and the hatred of others. Perhaps this was what war meant: understanding nothing.

Sometimes, my thoughts turned to Laure. I wanted to write to her, but then I gave up on the idea. I didn't know what to say, everything seemed so muddled up. I was waiting for things to improve, and then I could tell her all about it in a long letter to make her smile, like before. But for the time being, our country was like a barefoot zombie walking over sharp stones, its parched tongue hanging out. We had grown used to the idea of dying at any moment. Death was no longer something distant and abstract. It was the banal face of our everyday existence. Living with this kind of clarity laid waste to what was left of our childhood.

Lockdown operations were increasing in Bujumbura. From dawn until dusk, explosions echoed through the neighborhood. The nights shone red with the glow of fires sending up thick smoke above the hills. We were so accustomed to the sound of machine-gun fire and the rattle of automatic weapons that we didn't bother sleeping in the hallway anymore. Lying on my bed, I could admire the spectacle of tracer bullets in the sky. In another time and another place, I'd have mistaken them for shooting stars.

I found silence far more nerve-racking than the sound of gunfire. Silence might signal the violence of the knife, or a nocturnal intrusion that caught you unawares. Fear had made itself at home inside my spinal cord, and it wasn't going anywhere. There were times when I trembled like a small, wet dog shivering with cold. I stayed shut away at home, not daring to venture out anymore. Occasionally, I crossed the street in haste, to borrow a new book from Madame Economopoulos. But I was back in no time, burying myself in the bunker of my imagination. In my bed, deep in my stories, I sought out more bearable realities, and those books—my friends—painted my days with light again. I told myself that one day the war would be over: I would look up from those pages, I would leave my bed and my bedroom, and Maman would be back, in her beautiful flowery dress, her head resting on Papa's shoulder, and

Ana would draw new red-brick houses with chimneys producing puffs of smoke, and fruit trees in the garden and big shiny suns, and the band of brothers would come to find me, so we could all head downriver, like in the old days, on a raft made from the trunk of a banana tree, navigating the Muha as far as the turquoise waters of the lake, before ending the day on the beach, laughing and playing like children.

But no matter how much hope I held out, my dreams were fettered by reality. The world and its violence were closing in on us a little more each day. Ever since our little gang had decided not to remain neutral, our street was no longer the haven of peace I longed for. My friends and everyone else would end up driving me out of my bunker.

29

THE CITY WAS IN LOCKDOWN. GANGS WERE BLOCKING
the main roads. Hatred was at large. A new dark day, another
one, was dawning in Bujumbura, and everyone was ordered to
remain at home. Shut away. Rumor had it that the anger levels
of the young Tutsi gangs controlling the town had ratcheted up
because, the previous day, rebel Hutus had burned alive some
Tutsi students at a gas station, in the interior of the country.
The Tutsi gangs had decided to take revenge on any Hutu who
dared to go outdoors. Papa had got in supplies for the best part
of a week. We were expecting some long days of waiting ahead.
Back from stocking up on books round at Madame Economopoulos's, I was pouring myself a large glass of milk curds
and looking forward to burrowing under the covers to devour
my books, when I heard Gino scratching at the kitchen door.

"What are you doing here?" I whispered, as I opened up.
"It's madness to be outside today."

"Stop freaking out all the time, Gaby! And hurry, something serious is up."

He didn't want to say any more, so I hastily put on my shoes.
I could hear Papa and Ana laughing at cartoons in the living
room. I slipped outside noiselessly and followed Gino, who
darted ahead. We took a shortcut, climbing over the fence and
cutting through the football pitch of the International School.

An opening in Gino's wire fencing meant we could sneak across his garden. I heard the eternal clickety-clack of his father's Olivetti. We leaped over the gate and took a right toward the far end of the *impasse*. It was deserted. Heading back up it, there wasn't a soul about as we passed in front of the closed kiosk, then the *cabaret*, turning left onto the patch of wasteland. It had become so overgrown you could no longer see the Combi from the road.

Just as we were about to open the hideout door, I had a bad feeling, something telling me to go back home and escape into the world of my books. But before I could listen to my misgivings, Gino slid open the door.

Armand was collapsed on the dusty seat of the VW, his clothes covered in blood. Violent sobbing racked his chest. Between two spasms, he let out a high-pitched groan. Frowning, Gino gritted his teeth and flared his nostrils in anger. "His father was ambushed yesterday evening, here on our street. Armand just got back from the hospital. His father died of his wounds today. It's over."

My legs buckled as I tried to grab hold of the headrest on the passenger seat. My head was spinning. Gino headed out of the van with a mean-looking expression and sat on an old tire full of stagnant water. He hid his face in his hands. I was speechless as I stared at Armand, whose tears kept coming, whose clothes were splattered with the blood of his father. A father he feared and revered in equal measure. People had come to murder him in cold blood on our street. In our peaceful haven. My last shred of hope had just vanished. This country was a death trap. I felt like a panicked animal caught up in a great bush fire. The final barrier had been smashed. War had burst in on us.

"Who did it?"

Armand shot me a hostile look.

"Hutus, of course! Who else? They had it all planned out. They waited for hours in front of our gates, with a basket of vegetables, passing themselves off as market gardeners from Bugarama. Then they stabbed him in front of the house, before setting off again, cool as you like, joking as they went. I was there, I saw everything."

Armand started crying again. Gino stood up and punched the van's bodywork several times. Out of control, he grabbed an iron bar and smashed the Combi's windscreen and rear-view mirrors. I watched him, distraught.

Francis turned up, looking stony-faced. He was wearing a bandana, like Tupac Shakur.

"Get moving," he said, "they're waiting for us."

Gino and Armand followed him without a word.

"Where are we going?" I asked.

"We're going to protect our neighborhood, Gaby," Armand replied, wiping his snot on the back of his hand.

In normal times, I'd have turned back. But the war was in our homes now, it was threatening us directly, together with our families. Armand's father had been murdered, and I no longer had a choice. Gino and Francis had criticized me for claiming these weren't my problems. They were vindicated by the facts. Death had just stolen into our street. There was no sanctuary left on earth. I lived here, in this city, in this country. There was nothing else for it. I put my best foot forward with our gang.

The *impasse* was silent. All we could hear was the crunch of gravel underfoot. The residents were stuck at home like toads in their holes. There wasn't a breath of wind. Nature had gone mute on us. A taxi was waiting at the end of the path, its engine running. Francis signaled to us to climb in. The driver wore sunglasses and had a gash on his left cheek. He was smoking marijuana. Francis greeted him with a fist-bump, Rasta-style. The car set off slowly. We had hardly gone a few meters when it stopped at the entrance to the Muha bridge. This was the main roadblock in the Kinanira district, guarded by young gang members from "The Invincibles." Behind a barbed-wire barricade, tires were burning. The thick black smoke issuing from them made it hard to gauge what was happening over on the bridge. A group of youths kept shouting, using baseball bats and large stones to attack a dark mass that was lying on the ground, inert. They appeared to be getting a thrill out of whatever they were doing. A few of the gang members spotted us and came over to meet us. Francis was on first-name terms with all of them. I recognized the man with the Kalashnikov, the one who had taken aim at us at the house.

"What the fuck are these two white kids doing here?" he asked, eyeing Gino and me.

"It's all right, Chief, they're with us, their mothers are Tutsi," Francis explained.

The man examined us sceptically. Then he rattled off some instructions to the others and climbed into the back of the car, next to us, his Kalashnikov between his legs, its magazine covered with stickers featuring Nelson Mandela, Martin Luther King, and Gandhi.

"Drive!" he commanded, banging the outside of the car door.

A youth pulled the barbed wire back off the road, and the car zigzagged carefully between the stones that littered the asphalt. Our eyes were smarting from the fumes of burning rubber, which also made us cough. Once we were level with the group that was all buzzed up on the bridge, the man with the Kalashnikov ordered the driver to stop. The gang members drew apart, grinning. A shiver ran down my spine. There, writhing at their feet, on the hot tar, was Attila, the Von Gotzens' black horse. In the very same spot where we had glimpsed the beast's shadow one stormy night, he now lay on the ground, his legs smashed, his body streaked with bloodied wounds. The youths had taken it out on the horse, which raised his head and looked in my direction, his sole remaining eye staring at me insistently. The guy with the Kalashnikov pointed the barrel of his gun out of the car window and the youths dispersed.

"*Bassi!*—that's enough!" he shouted, and the hail of bullets began. I nearly leaped out of my skin. Armand clung onto my shorts. The car set off again under the watchful gaze of those youths, visibly disappointed to have lost out on the highlight of their day.

When we reached the district of Kabondo, the driver turned off onto a potholed road that ran along the river.

"You the son of the ambassador who's just been killed?" enquired the guy with the Kalash.

Armand nodded without looking his way. The taxi had reached a rocky promontory overhanging the river. Huge kapok trees rooted in the red clayey soil surrounded the spot. We got out of the car to find there were other kids from our neighborhood there. Sons from good families, who I'd taken for law-abiding students, were armed with sticks and stones. A badly beaten man was writhing on the ground. The red laterite dust that covered his face and clothes had blended with the congealed blood from a fresh wound on his skull.

The guy with the Kalashnikov, whom the others were calling Clapton, grabbed Armand's arm and told him: "That Hutu is one of your father's assassins."

Armand didn't react. Clapton was the first to strike the man, and the others followed suit. The blows kept raining down. Caught up in the frenzy, Gino and Francis joined the pack. Just then, a motorbike pulled up at high speed and two men wearing helmets with visors dismounted.

"That's the boss," said Clapton, and everyone stopped the thrashing.

"Hey, guys, on your best behavior, it's the chief of 'The Die-hards' in person!" Francis declared proudly, turning toward Armand and me. "You're not gonna believe this!"

The passenger from the motorbike took off his helmet and handed it to the driver. When he saw me with the younger members of his gang, in full daylight during a lockdown, next to the victim groaning on the ground, I guess he couldn't be-lieve his eyes. The chief of "The Diehards" was none other than Innocent. And his face broke into a smile.

"Check it out, Gaby. Good to see you here."

I didn't reply. I just stood there, gritting my teeth and clenching my fists.

The gang members tied the victim's arms behind his back. Even though he was on the ground, he still put up a fight and it took several of them to immobilize him. In the scuffle, his identity card slipped out of his pocket, landing in the dust. Once they'd done their job, the men carried him over to the taxi. The driver with the scar produced a can of gasoline from the trunk and poured it over the car seats as well as on the hood, before closing the doors. The man didn't stop scream-ing, he was terrified, begging us to spare him. Innocent took a lighter out of his pocket. I recognized Jacques's Zippo, the one that'd been stolen from him on my birthday, shortly before the war, the silver one with stags engraved on it. Innocent offered the flame to Armand.

"It's your chance to avenge your father . . ."

Shaking his head, Armand shrank back, his face crumpled. At which point, Clapton walked up to Innocent.

"Chief," he suggested, "why don't you let the French kid prove he's one of us."

Innocent smirked, clearly surprised the idea hadn't already occurred to him. He came toward me, holding out the lit Zippo. My temples and heart were beating fit to burst. I scanned right and left, in search of help. I was trying to find Gino and Francis in the crowd, but when I caught their eye, I saw that they had the same blank faces as everyone else. Innocent wrapped my fingers around the lighter. He ordered me to throw it. The man in the taxi was staring intently at me. My ears were ringing. Everything was blurred. The kids in the gang were jostling me, hitting me, shouting in my face. I could hear the distant voices of Gino and Francis, the cries of wild animals, bursts of feverish hatred. Clapton was saying something about Papa and Ana. I was struggling to decipher his threats in the midst of the mayhem and all those calls for murder around me. Innocent lost his temper and said that if I didn't do it, he would personally make the journey to take care of my family. I pictured Papa and Ana lying peacefully on the couch, in front of the television. It was a vision of their innocence, of all the innocence in the world teetering on the edge of an abyss. And I felt sorry for them and also for myself, for the purity that is ruined by all-consuming fear, which transforms everything into wickedness, hatred, and death. Into lava. Everything around me grew hazy as the shouts of rage increased in volume. The man in the taxi was a horse that was almost dead. If there exists no sanctuary on earth, does one exist somewhere else?

I tossed the Zippo and the car caught fire. A giant inferno rose up into the sky, licking the uppermost branches of the kapok trees. The smoke escaped above the treetops. The man's cries pierced the air. I vomited on my shoes. I could dimly hear Gino and Francis congratulating me, and I felt them patting me on the back. Armand wept. Long after everybody else had left, he was still weeping, curled up like a fetus in the dust. We were alone in front of the burned-out wreck. The place was calm now, almost serene, with the river flowing below. It was practically dark. I helped Armand to his feet. We had to make our way home. Before leaving, I searched in the dust and ashes. I found the identity card of the man who had just died. The man I had killed.

30

Dear Laure,

I don't want to be a mechanic anymore. There's nothing left to fix, nothing left to save, nothing left to understand.

It's been snowing for days and nights over Bujumbura.

The doves have taken to the milky-white sky. Street children are decorating pine trees with red, yellow, and green mangoes. Farmers are schussing down the hills to the plains, hurtling along the wide avenues in toboggans made from wire and bamboo. Lake Tanganyika is a skating rink where albino hippopotamuses slide on their floppy bellies.

It's been snowing for days and nights over Bujumbura.

The clouds are sheep in a sky-blue field. The barracks of hospitals are empty. The prisons of schools have a thin coating of whitewash. The radio is broadcasting the sound of rare birdsong. The people have unfurled the white flag, and abandoned themselves to snowball fights in cotton fields. The sounds of laughter ring out, triggering avalanches of icing sugar in the mountains.

It's been snowing for days and nights over Bujumbura.

Leaning against a tombstone, I share a cigarette with old Rosalie over the shared grave of Alphonse and Pacifique. Six feet below the ice, I can hear them reciting love poems for the women they never had the time to love, humming songs of friendship for their fellow soldiers fallen in combat. The seasonal steam that escapes my mouth is blue, and it transforms into a myriad of white butterflies.

It's been snowing for days and nights over Bujumbura.

The drunks in the cabaret *are drinking warm milk from porcelain chalices in broad daylight. The vast sky is filled with stars that flash like the lights in Times Square. My parents fly over a sacramental moon, in the back of a sleigh drawn by frost-coated crocodiles. As they travel past, Ana throws handfuls of rice from humanitarian sacks.*

It's been snowing for days and nights over Bujumbura. Have I already told you that?

Snowflakes land delicately on the surface of things, coating infinity, their absolute whiteness permeating the world all the way to our ivory hearts. Heaven and hell no longer exist. Tomorrow, the dogs will go quiet. The volcanoes will sleep. People will return blank votes. And our ghosts in their wedding dresses will wander out into the wintry streets. We shall be immortal.

It's been snowing for days and nights now.

Bujumbura is immaculate.

Gaby

31

THE WAR IN BUJUMBURA INTENSIFIED. THE NUMBER of victims was so significant that the situation in Burundi had become international front-page news.

One morning, Papa found Prothé's corpse in the ditch in front of Francis's house, covered in stones. Gino said Prothé was just a houseboy, and he didn't understand what I was crying about. When the army attacked Kamenge, we lost all trace of Donatien. Had he been killed as well? Or had he fled the country, like so many others, in single file, a mattress on his head, a bundle of belongings in one hand, his children in the other, ants in the human tide flowing along the roads and tracks of Africa at this end of the twentieth century?

A minister dispatched from Paris arrived in Bujumbura with two repatriation planes for French nationals. School closed from one day to the next. Papa registered us for departure. A host family would be expecting Ana and me, over there, some-where in France, a nine-hour flight away from our home. Be-fore leaving, I went back to the Combi to pick up the telescope and return it to Madame Economopoulos. When it was time to say goodbye, she walked over to her library and tore out a page from one of her books. It was a poem. She would have preferred to copy it out, but there was no time left for copying out poems. I had to leave. She told me to keep the words safe, in memory of her, and that I would understand them later on, in a few years. Even after closing the heavy gates, I could hear her voice behind me, still lavishing me with never-ending wisdom: take care in the cold, look after your secrets, may you be rich in all that you read, in your encounters, in your loves, and never forget where you come from . . .

When we leave somewhere, we take the time to say good-bye: to the people, the things, and the places that we've loved. I didn't leave my country, I fled it. The door was wide open behind me as I walked away, without turning back. All I can remember is Papa's small hand waving from the balcony of the airport at Bujumbura.

I have lived for years in a country at peace, where every town has so many libraries that nobody notices them anymore. A country that's the way our street was, where the sound of war and the fury of the world reach us from a distance.

At night, it all comes back to me: the scent of the streets of my childhood, the calm rhythm of the afternoons, the reassuring sound of rain drumming on a metal roof. Sometimes I dream; I find myself walking up the path to my family home, by the road to Rumonge. The house hasn't moved. The walls, the furniture, the flowerpots, they're all there. And in my dreams about a country that has disappeared, I can hear the song of the peacocks in the garden, the far-off call of the muezzin.

In winter, I stare forlornly at the bare chestnut tree in the square below my block. In its place, I picture the mighty canopy of mango trees that kept my neighborhood cool. When I can't sleep, I open a small wooden box hidden under my bed, and the scent of memories washes over me as I look at the photos of Tonton Alphonse and Pacifique, at that picture of me in a tree taken by Papa one New Year's Day, the black-and-white beetle collected in the Kibira forest, Laure's perfumed letters, the voting ballots from the 1993 election that Ana and I found in the grass, a blood-stained identity card . . . I twist a braid of Maman's hair around my fingers and I read the poem by Jacques Roumain that Madame Economopoulos gave me on the day of my departure:

If you come from a country, if you are born there, as what might be called a native by birthright, well then, that country is in your eyes, your skin, your hands, together with the thick hair of its trees, the flesh of its soil, the bones of its stones, the blood of its rivers, its sky, its flavor, its men and women . . .

I sway between two shores, and this is the disease of my soul. Thousands of kilometers separate me from my previous life. It's not the terrestrial distance that makes the journey long, but the time that has elapsed. I was from a place, surrounded by family, friends, acquaintances and by warmth. I have found that place again, but it is empty of those who populated it, who gave it life and body and flesh. The memories projected onto what is before my eyes are futile. I used to think I was exiled from my country. But, in retracing the steps of my past, I have understood that I was exiled from my childhood. Which seems so much crueler.

I have found our street again. Twenty years later. It's changed. The great tall trees of the neighborhood have been razed to the ground. The sun crushes the days. Breezeblock walls topped with broken bottles and barbed wire have replaced the colorful bougainvillea hedges. The impasse *has been reduced to a gloomy, dusty corridor, its anonymous residents shut away in their houses. Only Armand still lives there, in the large friendly white-brick house at the end. His mother and sisters have scattered to the four corners of the world, from Canada to Sweden, via Belgium. When I ask him why he didn't follow them, he replies with his legendary humor: "Each to their own asylum! Political for those who leave, psychotic for those who stay."*

Armand has become a strapping man, a senior executive at a commercial bank. He has developed a paunch and responsibilities. On the evening of my return, he insists on taking me to our old local haunt, the cabaret. *"We'll go to the trendy places later, but first of all I want you to immerse yourself in the real country, direct and with no transfer." The little shack is still there, with the parched flamboyant tree in front of it, the moon casting its shadow onto the beaten earth. Its tiny flowers move weakly in the evening breeze. The* cabaret *welcomes talkers and the taciturn, force-fed on newspapers and disillusionment. In the same darkness as before, the customers empty their hearts and their bottles. I sit on a beer rack, next to Armand. He gives me sketchy news about Francis, who has become a pastor in an evangelical church. The twins and Gino? They're somewhere in Europe, but he hasn't tried contacting them. Neither have I. Why would we?*

He insists that I tell him about the life Ana and I led, on our arrival in France. I don't dare complain, imagining what he must have experienced during the fifteen years of war that followed our departure. But I do confide in him, with some embarrassment, that my sister doesn't want to hear about Burundi ever again. We fall quiet. I light a cigarette. The flame illuminates our faces with fleeting crimson. The years have passed, we avoid certain subjects. Such as the death of my father, who was ambushed on the road to Bugarama, a few days after our departure. We don't talk about the murder of Armand's father, either, or everything that followed. Some wounds don't heal.

In the darkness of the cabaret, *I feel as if I'm journeying backward. The customers indulge in the same conversations, the same hopes, the same ramblings as before. They talk about the forthcoming elections, about the peace agreements, about fears of a new civil war, about their disappointments in love, about the rising price of sugar and gasoline. The only thing that's new: occasionally I hear a mobile phone ringing to remind me that the times really have*

*changed. Armand removes the cap from a fourth bottle. We laugh
beneath the rust-colored moon as we recall our childhood follies,
our happy days. And I rediscover a small part of that eternal Burundi I thought had disappeared forever. I am pleasantly comforted
by the sensation of homecoming. In the dark, bathed in the rustling
whispers of the other drinkers, I am trying to make out a strange
reedy voice, in the distance, it's like a sound memory echoing inside
me. Is it the effect of the alcohol? I focus. Whatever that voice
evoked has gone now. We crack open a new round of beers. Armand asks me why I've returned. I tell him about the telephone
call I received several months earlier, on my birthday, informing
me of the death of Madame Economopoulos. She breathed her last
during her siesta, one autumn afternoon, facing the Aegean Sea,
with a novel on her lap. Was she dreaming of her orchids?*

*"I came to collect the trunks of books she left for me, here in
Bujumbura."*

*"So you came back for a pile of books?" Armand bursts out
laughing. And so do I, as the absurdity of this project dawns on
me. We keep talking. He tells me about the coup that followed my
departure, about the economic sanctions endured by the country,
the long years of war, the influx of new money, the local mafias,
the independent media, the NGOs that employ half the city, the
evangelical churches flourishing everywhere, the ethnic conflict
that has gradually disappeared from the political arena. That voice
murmurs again inside my ear. I grab Armand's arm. "Can you
hear it?" I gasp. I bite my lip. I tremble. Armand puts his hand on
my shoulder. "I didn't know how to tell you, Gaby. I wanted you
to find out for yourself. She's been coming here every evening, for
years . . ." That voice, a voice from beyond the grave, cuts me to
the quick. It mutters something about stains on the floor that won't
go. I jostle the shadows, stumble against a bottle rack, grope in the
dark until I reach the back of the shack. Curled up on the floor,*

over in the corner, she is sucking home-brewed alcohol through a straw. Here she is, after twenty years that have taken the toll of fifty on her unrecognizable body. I lean toward the old lady. I have the feeling she recognizes me, from the way she is staring at me in the glow of the lighter I hold up to her face. With untold tenderness, Maman puts her hand delicately on my cheek: "Is that you, Christian?"

I'm still not sure what I'm going to do with my life. For the time being, I plan on staying here, looking after Maman, waiting for her to feel better.

Day breaks and I want to write. I don't know how this story will end. But I do remember how it all began.

About the Author

GAËL FAYE was born in 1982 in Burundi to a French father and Rwandan mother. In 1995, after the outbreak of the civil war and the Rwandan genocide, the family moved to France. An author, a songwriter, and a hip-hop artist, he released his first solo album, *Pili Pili sur un croissant au beurre,* in 2013. *Small Country* is his first novel. A bestseller in France, it has been awarded numerous literary prizes, among them the Prix Goncourt des Lycéens, and is being published in thirty territories worldwide.